THE
PIRATE KING
COLLECTION

PART 1

With special thanks to Michael Ford, Allan Frewin Jones and Elizabeth Galloway

www.beastquest.co.uk

ORCHARD BOOKS
338 Euston Road, London NW1 3BH
Orchard Books Australia
Level 17/207 Kent St, Sydney, NSW 2000

A Paperback Original
First published in Great Britain in 2011
This collection published in Great Britain in 2013

A CIP catalogue record for this book is available from
the British Library.

ISBN 978 1 40833 000 5

Printed and bound by CPI Group (UK) Ltd, Croydon, CR0 4YY

The paper and board used in this paperback are natural recyclable
products made from wood grown in sustainable forests. The
manufacturing processes conform to the environmental regulations of
the country of origin.

Orchard Books is a division of Hachette Children's Books,
an Hachette UK company

www.hachette.co.uk

BALISK
THE WATER
SNAKE

BY ADAM BLADE

ORCHARD

THE

WESTERN OCEAN

THE FOREST
OF FEAR

THE V

THE RUBY DESERT

SPIN

*T*remble, warriors of Avantia, for a new enemy stalks your land!

I am Sanpao, the Pirate King of Makai! My ship brings me to your shores to claim an ancient magic more powerful than any you've encountered before. No one can stand in my way, especially not that pathetic boy, Tom, or his friends. Even Aduro cannot help you this time. My pirate band will pillage and burn without mercy, and my Beasts will be more than a match for any hero in Avantia.

Pirates! Batten down the hatches and raise the sails. We come to conquer and destroy!

Sanpao, the Pirate King

PROLOGUE

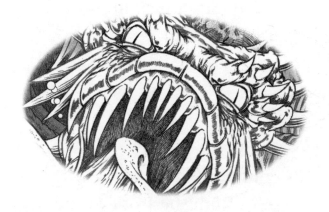

The sun beat down on across Leo's back. The old fisherman let the oars drop from his hands and he stood up. As the sea swell lifted and lowered his little boat, he gazed back to the east. He searched for any sign of the Avantian coast, but the sea stretched all the way to the horizon.

Further out than I've ever been, he thought grimly.

He turned west, squinting into the sun. The air was hot and eerily still;

the sail hung limply from the mast. If the wind didn't pick up soon, he'd be drifting all night.

But that was the least of Leo's worries. He picked up his flask and poured the last few drops of water into his mouth.

His empty catch-basket seemed to mock him from the front of the boat.

"I don't even have a good catch to show for my day's fishing!" he grumbled.

For years the coastal waters had teemed with fish, but in the last few days the shoals had all but vanished.

It's almost as if the fish are hiding from something, he thought with a shiver of fear.

Leo sat down heavily on the rowing bench, ready to take up the oars again in his blistered hands. His niece, Elenna, would start to worry if he wasn't back by sunset.

Poor Elenna, he thought as he rowed. *A girl like that shouldn't be stuck at home.* Her bow and arrow had hung on her bedroom wall ever since she'd returned from her latest adventures with Tom.

Whoosh! A large wave slapped against the side of the hull, rocking the boat. Leo jolted in his seat and turned.

"A ship!" he mumbled.

A huge vessel carved through the dark blue waves. She sat high in the water. Three masts rose from the deck. The one in the centre seemed more roughly hewn than the others, and was slightly bent, almost like the branch of some huge tree. But the strangest sight was the blood-red sails. They billowed, filling with wind, driving the ship onwards. Leo frowned. *But there's no breeze*, he thought.

A single flag trailed and whipped from the odd, central mast. On a black background, it showed what looked like the outline of a Beast's skull, with horns and long, crooked

teeth. *Is it some sort of warship?* Leo wondered. The vessel didn't look like anything in King Hugo's small navy that he had seen before.

Leo waved his arms wildly and shouted, "Over here! Please, help me!"

Even though the ship was still some fifty boat-lengths away, his own craft suddenly lurched. He tripped over, landing on his knees with a cry, and clung to the edge of his vessel. Leo didn't understand – the swell wasn't bad enough to knock him from his feet...

He stared into the water. There was something down there!

A dark shadow, bigger than any shark, drifted beneath the boat with menacing silence.

Leo scrambled to the other side of

his ship, just as the creature broke the surface. He fought the scream that rose in his throat as he saw the snake-like body. Glittering and muscular, the Beast rolled out of the water, sunlight scattering off its silver scales.

Rising up, the monster faced Leo with a head almost as big as his boat. Horns jutted from the head in all directions, and its yellow eyes narrowed to slits. The Beast rose higher still, blocking out the sun. With a hiss, it shot towards Leo.

Leo dived into the water to escape being crushed to death, and heard the crunch as his fishing boat was smashed into splinters. Under the water's surface, he saw the wreckage of his boat sinking. Panic drove the air from his lungs. His heart thudded in terror. The Beast was coming for him, twisting through the water, mouth gaping to reveal deadly fangs. Was this the last thing Leo would ever see?

CHAPTER ONE

A WAITING GAME

Tom threw aside his blanket. He stared out through the open window onto a rectangle of night sky.

"It's no use," he whispered.

In the next chamber, he could hear Uncle Henry snoring softly. Tom had tried everything – counting through every Beast he'd ever fought, lying on his front, on his side, flipping onto his back. He'd even tried sleeping on the bare floorboards, to remind himself of the many nights spent in the wilderness on his Quests. Nothing worked – he couldn't get to sleep.

"And nothing will work while my mother's lost in a strange land," he muttered.

In some ways, the last Quest in Tavania had been successful. He and Elenna had restored six Beasts to their rightful homes and he'd managed to bring the Evil Wizard Malvel back to Avantia, where he was now imprisoned in King Hugo's dungeon.

It wasn't worth it, Tom thought, his frustration mounting. They'd left his mother, Freya, in Tavania, and Elenna's wolf, Silver – a loyal companion on so many Quests.

How am I supposed to sleep when I've abandoned them?

Tom walked to the window and gazed out. He was sure that Elenna felt the same.

Following their return, the Good Wizard Aduro had told them to go back to their homes – Tom to his aunt and uncle in Errinel, and Elenna to her uncle Leo, a fisherman on the western shore. Aduro had said he'd wanted them both to recuperate after their latest adventures, and that he would do his best to find a way to bring the others home. But Tom couldn't just sit around waiting.

"I have to do something!" he said.

He picked up his shield and sword. He began a series of drills, attacking and backing off from imaginary foes and remembered Beasts: he lunged, thrust and sliced; he ducked, weaved, and leapt; all in determined silence so he wouldn't wake his aunt and uncle.

Soon sweat began to prick across his skin. Maybe if he could tire himself out, he'd at last be able to get some sleep.

Suddenly, the wall in front of him seemed to shimmer, the rough stone melting and blurring. Tom gripped his sword tighter, ready to meet the intruder, and lifted his shield with its six tokens across his body. A shape appeared, vague at first, then growing solid. Tom recognised the floppy cone of Aduro's hat and lowered his shield as the Good Wizard took on his familiar shape.

Aduro peeled away from the wall, and stood in the room with Tom.

Only the slight golden haze
surrounding the wizard's form told
Tom this was only a vision.

"Do you have news of my

21

mother?" Tom asked immediately.

Aduro shook his head. "You must have patience, Tom."

Tom knew in his heart that the wizard was right, but this did not soothe his restlessness.

"Is there nothing I can do to help?" he asked.

"Not at the moment," said Aduro. "I have sent Taladon in search of something called the Tree of Being. It may have the power to open a portal into Tavania."

Tom's heart lifted. "Where is this Tree?"

"Nobody knows for sure," said Aduro. "Legend tells us that the tree doesn't remain in one place, it's forever moving about our kingdom."

It didn't sound like any tree Tom had ever heard of. "Where is my father now? I'll go with him."

"This is not your Quest, Tom," said Aduro.

"But two warriors are stronger than—"

Aduro raised a hand. "Freya is dear to Taladon, too," he said. "You must let him fight alone."

Before Tom could protest further, the vision of Aduro melted into the stone wall and Tom found himself alone again.

A rustle outside made his skin tingle. He heard the sound of a twig splintering underfoot. Could it be an intruder? Or a fox maybe, after his aunt's chickens?

Tom crept to the window. He heard the snap of a bow-string, then – *whoosh!* An arrow thudded into the wooden window frame.

CHAPTER TWO

TO THE CASTLE

Tom peered out of the window, ready to duck out of sight if the attacker shot again.

Sitting in the crook of a branch on a nearby tree he made out the figure of a girl, silhouetted against the moon. She waved.

Elenna!

Tom ran across his bedroom and pulled open the door with a creak.

He crept barefoot through the kitchen of the cottage and out into the summer night. As he rushed over to the tree, Elenna slipped from the branch and landed, silent as a cat, in the grass. Tom had never been so glad to see his friend. She grinned.

"What are you doing here?" he asked her.

"I can't wait around any longer!" she whispered. "Silver's stuck in another world. Your mother is, too. Every day that passes is a wasted opportunity to rescue them!"

Tom told Elenna about Aduro's visit, and the Tree of Being.

"If it's out there, then Taladon needs our help," said Tom.

A frown passed over Elenna's face. "I agree, but if we can't find this tree—"

"I don't care!" interrupted Tom. "It's my mother we're talking about, and our friend."

"You're right," she said. "Aduro *has* to help us!"

"Wait by the stables," said Tom. He rushed back indoors, more noisily than before, to collect his sword and shield. He was too excited to care about tiptoeing around! As he sat on his bed lacing his boots, Uncle Henry stumbled into the room, rubbing his eyes.

"Is something the matter, Tom? I heard… Are you going somewhere?"

Tom stood up. "I can't say now, Uncle, but you have to trust me. I might be able to help my mother."

Uncle Henry looked worried, but gave a nod. "I understand. Do what you must, but be careful, you hear?"

Tom smiled. "Give my love to Aunt Maria," he said.

He met Elenna at the stables, where she was already saddling Storm. The stallion neighed and tossed his head.

"Looks like he's ready for another Quest," said Tom, as he tightened the straps under Storm's belly. He put a foot in the stirrup and threw himself into the saddle.

"Just the three of us this time," said Elenna.

"Not for long, hopefully," Tom said, reaching down to help her up. "We'll find Silver soon. We have to!"

Storm galloped all the way to King Hugo's castle. The brisk air cleared Tom's head and focused his mind on the challenge facing them: convincing Aduro to let them be

part of this Quest.

They arrived as dawn was painting
the sky with pink streaks from the
east. The pale stone of the
battlements and towers seemed to
gleam like gold, and sentries stood

guard on top of the walls. Storm's hooves clattered over the open drawbridge and into the central courtyard.

Tom left Storm with a stable-hand. "Take care of him, will you?" he asked.

The boy nodded, and Tom and Elenna raced up the spiral staircase of the turret leading to Aduro's chamber. Tom burst through the door without knocking.

The wizard stood in the centre of the room, his cloak gathered around him. He was uttering a low chant as he stared into a crystal globe. It glowed faintly, and Aduro's hands moved on either side as if controlling some hidden force. So mesmerized with what he was doing that he didn't notice Tom and Elenna.

"Greetings," said Tom.

The Good Wizard jerked his head up and smiled. With a hasty wave of his hand, the glowing orb faded. Tom caught a glimpse of something shimmering in its surface – the shape of a Beast skull.

"Greetings, young ones," said Aduro. "What an unexpected surprise!"

"We want to help," said Elenna. "Has Taladon found the Tree of Being yet?"

A look of anger creased the wizard's face. "I told you, this is not—"

A shout of alarm rose up from the courtyard below. "Fetch a physician! We have an injured man here!"

Tom and Elenna rushed to the window of the turret. A horse stumbled weakly across the centre

of the courtyard, while a groom tried
to grab its bridle. Across the horse's
back lay a man, his body limp and his
hands looped in the reins. The man's
head rested against the horse's mane,

and the back of his tunic was stained red. Tom recognised the chestnut stallion at once, and felt fear clutch his heart.

"Isn't that horse…?" Elenna began.

"Yes," said Tom, his voice cracking with dread. "Fleetfoot."

The blood-splattered man on the horse was Taladon.

CHAPTER THREE

A NEW ENEMY

Tom's blood turned to ice. He ran for
the door with Elenna close behind.

"Wait!" called Aduro.

Tom bounded out into the
courtyard. A small crowd of
stable-hands had gathered, and two
of them lowered Taladon from the
saddle, turning him over gently.

He can't be dead, thought Tom.
"Let me through!"

He gasped when he saw Taladon's face. One eye was swollen shut and his lips were cracked and dry. From a cut on his forehead, fresh blood leaked across his cheek and nose. Tom crouched beside his father, and Taladon moaned softly.

Aduro stood over them, looking on gravely and panting a little after rushing from his chamber.

"What happened?" Tom asked.

Taladon moved his lips, but at first no sound came out.

"Water!" said Tom.

One of the grooms handed down a flask, and Tom tipped a little of the liquid into his father's mouth.

"I found it," he croaked.

"The Tree of Being?" Aduro asked.

Taladon tried to nod. "I came so close, but I was attacked."

"Who did this to you?" asked Tom.

"By…" Taladon's eyes closed.

"Enough questions!" snapped Aduro.

"Father?" Tom said in panic.

Elenna placed two fingers to the side of Taladon's neck. "It's all right. His heart still beats."

"We need to get him to the infirmary," Tom said.

Aduro ordered the grooms to bring a stretcher. As Taladon was lifted up, something dropped from his hand.

"What is it?" asked Elenna.

Tom flattened out the square of rough cloth on the ground. It was dirty white, like sail cloth. In the centre of the square was a symbol he recognised – a Beast skull, staining the cloth red like a bloodstain. Tom looked at Aduro.

"Whose symbol is this?" he asked. "I saw it in the globe in your chamber."

The wizard lowered his eyes and shook his head. "I cannot say."

"Tom, there's something on the other side," said Elenna.

He turned the cloth over. In red lettering, a message was scrawled: *Death has arrived. Yours, Sanpao.*

Tom felt a shudder of dread. "Enough!" he said, standing and facing Aduro. "Why won't you tell us? Who is this Sanpao?"

"He's just a pirate," said Aduro. "No great threat to Avantia."

Tom could hardly believe what the wizard was saying. "No great threat? He almost killed my father!"

"You exaggerate," said Aduro. "Taladon's injuries will soon heal. He will be able to fight once more."

Tom thought he saw a flicker of guilt in the wizard's face. "No!" said Tom, more strongly than he intended. "I will fight this...this Sanpao! The Quest *must* pass to me."

"You mustn't let your anger take over," said Aduro.

Elenna placed a hand on Tom's arm. "Maybe Aduro's right," she said.

"Maybe you should leave this Quest to a more experienced warrior." She winked as she spoke.

Tom could see she wanted him to play along. Something wasn't right with Aduro's behaviour: Tom had never known him to be so unwilling to face up to Avantia's enemies.

"Yes," he said, raising his voice so that everyone could hear. "Perhaps we aren't strong enough for this Quest."

"I'm glad you see sense," said Aduro. He looked to the grooms, then pointed at Taladon. "Take this man to the king's physician, at once."

They obeyed, lifting Taladon on his stretcher. Aduro walked back to his turret. Elenna shrugged at Tom as if to say: *What's going on?*

As the stretcher-bearers passed,

Taladon suddenly came to and reached out with a hand, gripping his son's arm strongly. He raised his body slightly, gritting his teeth.

"Come close," he whispered, his eyes flickering to one side. It was almost as though Taladon didn't want anyone to hear. "Danger lies at sea," Taladon hissed. "Sanpao...he can control Beasts."

Tom's father sank back down again and was carried inside the palace.

"Are you all right?" asked Elenna.

Tom crumpled the sail-cloth in his fist.

"While there's blood in my veins," he said, "I won't rest until Sanpao is defeated. And I don't care if I have Aduro's permission or not."

CHAPTER FOUR

ANOTHER FRIEND LOST

The day had passed slowly, and when nightfall came, Tom and Elenna sneaked out to the stable. The stable-boy was sleeping on some straw, and they crept past him. Storm stayed silent as they fastened the saddle and bridle, then mounted him.

Tom squeezed Storm's flanks and the stallion moved quietly out of the

stables and towards the castle gates.
The stable-boy jerked awake.

"What—" he mumbled. "No!" He
stumbled to stand in front of Storm.

"Let us pass," said Tom.

"But you can't! Strict instructions
from Wizard Aduro."

"Tell him we overpowered you,"
said Tom. "One way or another,
we're going through those gates."

He lowered his hand to the hilt of
his sword, and the boy's eyes
widened. Tom hated using the threat,
but there was no time to waste. The
boy stepped aside, and Tom kicked
Storm into a canter. They surged
through the gates.

"Stop!" called a voice.

Tom tugged on Storm's reins, and
looked back towards the castle. On
the battlements stood Aduro. In one

hand he grasped his staff, and in the
other was a torch, trailing flames in
the night breeze.

"How dare you disobey me!" he
roared. The torch cast orange light
over his twisted features.

"We're only trying to help!"
shouted Elenna.

Aduro cackled, an evil sound. "You
will pay a price for your treachery!"
he bellowed.

"We're not the traitors!" Elenna

called back with anger in her voice.

Aduro pointed his staff, and from the tip a blast of purple light spun towards them. Tom didn't have time to lift his shield, and his body shuddered as the magic entered him. When he opened his eyes, he was still seated in Storm's saddle, unharmed. He checked Elenna, but she'd been protected behind him.

"I don't understand," he muttered. "Nothing happ—"

"Your belt!" Elenna gasped.

Tom glanced to his waist. The precious jewelled belt, which held the tokens gathered on his Quests against Malvel's Beasts, had vanished. In its place, a wide sash was fastened around his waist. It looked as if it had been made with some type of animal hide, patchy with mangy fur.

Tom hardly had time to question
what had happened. If Aduro was
their enemy now, the sooner they
put distance between themselves and
him the better. He turned Storm
around again, away from the castle.
Over his shoulder he called back to
Aduro: "Belt or no belt, I won't stand
by while Avantia is threatened!"

"And we won't come back until Sanpao's gone for good!" shouted Elenna.

Tom nudged Storm's flanks and they galloped off into the night.

They headed towards the coast. Taladon's last words were a clue to where to head, and surely any pirates would have to come from the sea. But the Western Ocean was three days' ride away.

"It's a good job we've done so much travelling in Avantia," said Tom. "The quickest way is through the Forest of Fear."

Tom kept Storm at a gallop across the Grassy Plains to the edge of the forest. As the pink of dawn streaked across the sky, Avantia seemed at peace. Tom checked behind them every time they reached high ground, but there was no sign of riders in pursuit. The only person they passed was a woodcutter, leading an empty cart with a nodding donkey.

"What has happened to Aduro?" Tom asked as they trotted into the forest.

"He seems more like Malvel than the Good Wizard of Avantia," said Elenna.

Tom touched the sash, and began to pull it off.

"What do you think that's for?" asked Elenna.

"I don't know, but I don't like it," said Tom, giving up on ripping it off. "It's probably some sort of dirty trick."

Tom felt Elenna grip him a little tighter. "We'll have to be extra careful," she said.

"My father said Sanpao could control Beasts," said Tom. "We need to keep our eyes peeled – they could be lurking anywhere."

"I wish we had Silver with us," said Elenna, peering between the trees. "His nose would be perfect for finding our way."

Tom leant forward in the saddle to hack at overhanging branches. But as the sun rose higher, they met no surprises. The birds sang in the trees and clouds scudded across the blue sky. The kingdom seemed untroubled. Soon the trees began to thin out.

"We're nearing the other side," said Tom.

They passed beyond the wild reaches of the forest to more ordered rows of trees, with small huts and

fences. Apples hung from the
branches.

"An orchard," Tom said. "We must
be near a village." He pulled on
Storm's reins, and tensed.

"What is it?" asked Elenna

Tom pointed through the orchard
to a tree. A section of trunk had been
torn away in the rough shape of
a Beast's skull. *Just like the one I saw
in Aduro's crystal orb*, thought Tom.
Beneath the mark, more bark had
been gouged out to spell the message:
Death has arrived.

"We must be close," whispered
Elenna. "Do you think—"

A piercing scream cut her short.

CHAPTER FIVE

A PIRATE RAID

"That way!" hissed Elenna, pointing through the trees. They dismounted Storm and tethered him to a branch.

"He'll be safe here," Tom whispered. A cry of "*help*" drifted through the trees.

With their weapons clutched in their hands, Tom and Elenna darted between the trees into the outskirts of the village as the shouts of alarm grew louder. Tom saw a terrified villager with a cut to his forehead running between two buildings. He sprinted towards him, but Elenna drew him back in the shade of a large wooden apple-press for making juice.

"We can't just rush in," she said. "Let's see what we're facing first."

Tom peered around the press into the village square. Tanned, burly men in heavy leather boots, wearing sleeveless jerkins over muscled torsos, tramped across the square, cutlasses drawn.

"Sanpao's pirates?" asked Elenna.

"They must be," said Tom.

They wore billowing trousers that tapered at the ankles. One passed close and Tom ducked back out of sight. The man wore leather belts around his waist, looped through buckles crafted from polished bone.

"Look at their hair!" whispered Elenna.

Each pirate had the front portion of his head shaved. Some tied their locks in long ponytails that trailed down their backs. Others wore the plait looped around their necks.

Across their bulging forearms, each had a tattoo of the Beast skull. *Sanpao's mark*, Tom thought.

"There are too many to take on," Tom said. "We need a distraction."

In the centre of the village square stood a mighty oak tree. Two pirates, one on each side, were swinging axes in turn at the trunk. The leaves shook with every blow. But why were they cutting down the tree?

It's no use us storming in, thought Tom. *Innocent villagers will get hurt.* He looked around. The apple-press was a tall wooden structure, on top of which rested a steel vat. Tom wondered if he had the strength to topple it.

The tree in the middle of the square groaned, leaning dangerously.

"Timber!" The tree leaned to one

side, and with a horrible crunching sound, split at the base. The trunk toppled, crashing through the roof of a cottage and sending a huge cloud of sawdust and leaves into the air.

The pirates gathered around. "So much for magic," one snarled.

"I told you it wasn't the Tree of Being," said the one with an axe, wiping the sweat from his brow. "What a waste of time! We need that tree and its portals if we're to raid the riches of every kingdom we find."

So that's why they are here, Tom thought. *These men are looking for the same thing as us – the Tree of Being. But why?* Tom couldn't believe these tough men were on a quest to help anyone.

"Well, you can tell Sanpao we've failed!" said the pirate's friend.

The man with the axe went pale.

Tom looked at Elenna. "If the pirates get to the tree first, it looks like they'll hack it down," he said.

"And we won't be able to rescue Freya and Silver," Elenna added.

"Help me," said Tom, leaning his weight against the vat. Elenna strained with him, but it hardly budged. Tom dug his heels into the ground and threw his back against the wooden structure. Elenna grimaced beside him, and beads of sweat appeared on her forehead. The vat began to tip. Tom's muscles burned, but he didn't let up until he felt the weight of the vat topple.

"Eh? Look out!" shouted one of the pirates.

Tom almost fell as the vat toppled over. A wave of slippery apple pulp splashed across the square. The pirates skidded as they ran away, losing their footing with cries of surprise. They landed with a splash, flailing in the sticky juice of crushed apple.

Tom and Elenna charged out from their hiding place.

When the tattooed lead pirate saw them, his eyes widened in surprise. He pointed his dripping cutlass.

"Carve them to pieces!" he ordered.

Elenna loosed an arrow, making all the pirates duck. She strung another, and this one buried itself in the thigh of one of Sanpao's men. He screamed in pain.

"They're only children!" shouted the lead pirate.

Tom took a blow to his shield and lashed out, sending the pirate's cutlass spinning from his hand. He kicked another in the gut, who staggered into three others, tumbling them all into the apple pulp.

"Back to the ship!" ordered the lead man, staggering away. "We'll live to fight another day!"

The ship? thought Tom. *But we're still a day's ride from the sea!*

Soon the pirates were fleeing the village. Tom helped up one of the villagers, and Elenna went to check on an old man who had been struck across the cheek.

The villagers gathered around Tom.

"Thank you," gasped the man Tom had helped up. He mopped at his bleeding nose with his sleeve. "Whoever you are, you saved us. Others have not been so fortunate." He shared a nervous glance with the other villagers.

"Go on," urged Tom.

"We've heard these pirates have been wreaking havoc across West Avantia – north of here," he said.

"Then we must go," Tom said.

"Stay on your guard."

The man slapped him on the back. "Good luck, and thank you."

Tom and Elenna walked quickly back to the orchard. He unlooped Storm's reins and caught sight of the tree marking again.

"He won't get away with this," Tom muttered darkly. But at least he and Elenna had been given a glimpse of who their enemy was – the leader of a cruel, ruthless group of men.

Once they were in the open plains again, Tom followed the setting sun westward. The air turned colder with the winds coming off the sea, and he tasted the salt tang on the air. Elenna pointed out that they weren't far from the village where she lived with her Uncle Leo, and suggested they head in that direction.

They crossed the shifting dunes that led to the coast, and soon the silver ocean appeared on the horizon. Elenna pointed to some fisherman's shacks down near the shore. "That's my Uncle Leo's cottage," she said.

They cantered the remaining distance to the shack, and Elenna rushed inside. Tom found her standing in an empty room beside a table. She held a piece of paper.

"What's the matter?" he said.

She frowned. "This is the note I left when I came to find you," she said. "Four days ago!"

"What could it mean?" asked Tom.

"Well, he's either gone away, or..."

"What?"

Elenna turned to him. "Or, he never returned from his fishing trip. My uncle might be lost at sea!"

CHAPTER SIX

THE TREE OF BEING

"Uncle Leo's the only family I've got left," said Elenna.

"Come on," Tom said. "Perhaps the other fishermen know something."

Elenna nodded. Tom could see she was being brave, but he knew all too well that no one could survive adrift in the ocean without water for four days. Outside the shack, two fishermen were tying up their boat to a jetty. Elenna called out to them.

"Have you seen Leo?" she asked.

Both men shook their heads. The older of the two, who had a shaggy white beard and a bald, sunburned head, tipped the basket he was holding to show there was nothing inside.

"Not seen Leo for days now," he said. "There's no fish out there. Maybe he went down the coast, hoping for better luck."

"Why are there no fish?" asked Tom.

The two fishermen shared a furtive glance. "Now don't start that again..." said the younger one.

"Start what?" asked Elenna.

"Father thinks he saw something

out there," said the younger man.

"Something big..." muttered the old man.

Tom looked to Elenna. *A Beast!*

"I tell you one thing for certain," said the older man, "something's not right under the waves."

Dusk set in quickly, turning the sea black. The moon picked out the silver crests of the waves.

"Let's light a fire," Tom suggested.

While Elenna found some oats for Storm, Tom went further up the beach to collect driftwood. The fishermen offered him some dried fish and bread before retiring to their tiny shack. As they sat eating beside the fire, Tom saw Elenna looking out to sea, her eyes shining with tears. He hated to think that Leo had met Sanpao. Or worse, a Beast...

"Don't give up hope," he urged his friend.

"I know," she said. "It's just that I couldn't bear to lose him... Not after—" she paused. "It's late. Let's get some rest. Maybe the morning will bring some more clues."

As Tom lay down beside the fire, he admired his friend's bravery. He tried not to think of his father, lying injured in the palace infirmary. Or his mother, trapped in a foreign land. He drifted into troubled sleep.

Tom woke later with a start, the sweat cooling on his skin. It was still night, but the first hints of dawn washed the sky a blue-grey. The fire had died to just a glow of smouldering orange wood.

"Are you all right?" asked Elenna, stirring.

"I think so," he said. He felt a vibration in the ground, and the embers shifted.

"An earthquake!" he said, springing up.

Storm snorted wildly as fresh flames spluttered then died. The ground lurched and Tom lost his footing, falling in the sand. His eyes fixed on the centre of the fire, where the ground seemed to split apart. With a deep rumble, a spike of bark sprouted, thrusting up and scattering hot coals and sand. It rose, higher and higher like a wooden column, until it towered twenty times taller than a man.

Tom found his voice. "Do you think—" he began.

"It must be," gasped Elenna. "The Tree of Being!"

It was nothing like Tom had imagined. 'The Tree of Death' would have been a better way to describe it. The black bark that covered its trunk was cracked and diseased, and the

stunted branches had no leaves or buds. Tom circled the tree with Elenna, looking up. The branches drooped, ready to snap. A smell like rotten cabbage filled Tom's nostrils. On one side, where a branch had obviously once been, a round patch leaked sap, weeping like an open wound. There was no sign of any portal.

"If this was once a gateway to another world, I'm not sure it is any more," said Tom.

"Look!" said Elenna, pointing to where he'd been sleeping a moment ago.

There, in the sand, lay his shield. There seemed to be a golden glow around its rim.

"Why's it doing that?" Elenna asked.

Tom picked up the shield carefully, and carried it closer to the trunk. As he did so, it glowed brighter.

"I've always wondered why the shield was so strong," he said. "Maybe the wood came from this tree!"

"Then perhaps it still has some power," said Elenna. "It clearly has a magic connection with your shield. We have to stop Sanpao before he can get near the tree."

"We need a boat," Tom said. "We must meet him head on – out at sea."

He ran across the beach to the fisherman's shack and pounded on the door with his fist. Elenna followed him, leading Storm. The older man opened the door and peered out. "Can we borrow your boat?" Tom asked.

"No point us having it, is there?" said the man, shrugging. "Just bring it back in one piece."

"We'll leave our horse with you as a sign of trust," said Tom. He ruffled Storm's mane. "Don't worry, we'll be back for you soon."

Storm whinnied softly as Elenna climbed into the boat, scrambling over the pile of nets and fishing spears. Tom pushed the little vessel across the sand until they were ankle deep in water, then he hopped on board. Tom and Elenna took an oar each, and began to heave long strokes. The morning sun peeped over the horizon, leaving a golden trail across the Western Ocean.

Elenna, more experienced at sea, hoisted the sail to catch the breeze, whilst Tom scanned the coastline.

If they could get to Sanpao before he even made land, perhaps they could turn them back to where they came from without any bloodshed.

Soon they were cutting through the water by the power of the wind alone. Tom shielded his eyes against the sun, but saw no sign of any life on the waves. Then he spied a shape on the horizon.

"Over there!" he shouted.

Elenna turned excitedly. "Is it my uncle?"

It was a ship – a floating fortress! The craft was huge, with three giant masts and red sails tied with rigging. Spikes jutted from the gunwales and a poop-deck rose at the rear. It stalked towards them through the water, and gradually a familiar shape appeared on its highest flag.

"The Beast Skull!" Tom gasped.
"It's Sanpao's ship."

CHAPTER SEVEN

THE PIRATE KING

The swell from the mighty pirate ship threatened to capsize them, but Tom gripped each side to steady himself. Close up, he saw that the central mast differed from the other two. It wasn't smoothly carved and straight, but twisted slightly in the middle. Along its length were several scars where other, smaller branches had been hacked away. In other places the branches had sprouted, and were lined with golden leaves.

"It's still alive!" said Elenna.

"That must be the missing branch from the Tree of Being," Tom said, remembering the weeping patch from the tree on the beach. "How could they do such a thing? Does it steal the tree's magic?" He stood up in the rocking boat. "Where's the scoundrel, Sanpao?" he shouted.

The snarling pirates on deck parted, and a huge man stepped forward to the rail of the raised poop-deck. He wore the same sort of clothes as the raiding party Tom had seen in the village, but his garments were all black. The only sign of colour was a sparkle around his waist, hidden mostly in the folds of his clothing. He had a broad chest, and tattoos

climbed up his thick arms. His face
was lined with scars, and his left eye
drooped slightly with an area of pink,
scarred flesh, perhaps from a burn.
His oiled ponytail was studded with
darts.

He drew a curved cutlass from his
scabbard, and held it aloft. Tom
shuddered when he saw the edge

was lined with serrations like shark teeth.

"Did someone ask for Sanpao, the Pirate King?" he bellowed.

"I did!" Tom called back.

Sanpao tipped back his head in deep laughter. "And who might you be, boy?"

"I'm Tom," he shouted. "And you almost killed my father, Taladon."

"I've heard stories about you!" said Sanpao. "Your little friend there must be Elenna."

"His 'little friend' is a match for any of your crew!" she shouted back.

"I guess your nag couldn't join you at sea," continued Sanpao. "And the mutt… Oh, I forgot, he's lost, isn't he? Lost with your dear mother, far, far away!"

Tom's blood boiled.

"How does he know so much about us?" whispered Elenna.

The Pirate King laughed. "I have my sources. By the way, how is my new friend Aduro?"

There was something in the way Sanpao said 'new friend' that made Tom uneasy. Images of the ghostly skull floating in the wizard's crystal ball filled his mind. "Have you done something to him?" Tom asked, snatching up an oar to bring them closer to the pirate ship.

Sanpao's eyes gleamed with triumph. "Aduro grows old," he said. "Weak. Bewitching him was easy!"

"You won't get away with this!" Tom cried.

Sanpao rolled his eyes. "My wizard said you never give up," he said. "If I have to kill you both to get to the Tree of Being, so be it. My Beast is hungry!" He stooped to the deck and straightened up, gripping a conch shell as big as Tom's head. He raised it to his lips, and blew. The noise that came out sounded like a war-horn, and lingered on the still air.

Elenna screamed as a man in rags was shoved forwards between the pirates on deck. "Uncle Leo!"

Two pirates extended a plank over the edge of the ship, and pushed Elenna's uncle onto it. Sanpao strode across the deck and levelled his cutlass towards Leo's throat.

"Time for a final bath, old man."

Leo edged slowly along the plank, which wobbled perilously. Tom felt his stomach sink – Leo was going to be fed to a Beast!

"Don't worry, uncle!" shouted

Elenna. "We'll rescue..."

The words died in her throat as, beneath their craft, the water began to swirl. A shadow moved beneath the waves. For a moment, even the pirates on the deck stopped their jeering. The shadow grew as the Beast surged towards the surface, and Tom pushed Elenna from the side as it burst from the waves. From the sodden boards, he gazed in horror as the Beast rose into the air. The creature's fins were lined with sharp claws and deadly spikes stuck out from its neck. The Beast lashed its scaly, tapered tail into the water, showering them with brine, before crashing into the sea again.

Tom felt Elenna clutch at his arm, and he knew she was thinking the same thing as him. Sanpao's stolen

magic must have been extremely powerful, if he could control Beasts, and use them as his greatest, fiercest servants.

Sanpao pressed the tip of his sword into Leo's back. "Get a move on!" he shouted. "Balisk the Water Snake must be fed!"

Leo's arms flailed, but Tom could see he was going to fall. "Please..." shouted Leo.

Balisk's jaws gaped, revealing needle-like teeth, as it roared with hunger.

CHAPTER EIGHT

A BEAST FROM THE DEEP

"No!" screamed Elenna.

Tom picked up a fishing spear from the boat and hurled it towards Leo with all his strength.

"Grab this!" he shouted.

Leo toppled off the plank as the spear thudded into the side of the pirate vessel. The old man managed to wrap his arms around the shaft, his legs dangling. The pirates shouted down curses.

With a roar, Balisk surged out of the water towards Elenna's uncle. Leo pulled up his legs with a wail, and the Beast's jaws snapped shut a fraction too short.

I have to tackle that monster, Tom thought, *before someone dies.*

With one foot on the edge of the

fishing boat, Tom launched himself off. He landed on the Beast's body just behind the horned head. He almost slid off the slippery scales, but managed to hold on to one of the fins. He gripped Balisk's flanks as if he was a wild horse. Balisk roared with fury.

The Beast thrashed in the water, threatening to tear Tom's arms from

their sockets. Tom managed to draw his sword and struck against Balisk's head with the flat of his blade. He landed a heavy blow, and for a moment the Beast's movements became sluggish.

Through the spray and churning waves, Tom saw that Elenna had sat on the side of the boat and was pulling closer to the pirate ship with both oars. Pirates were hurling daggers at Tom's friend. She ducked aside as the blades thunked into the boat's hull or scythed harmlessly into the water.

"Uncle Leo," she shouted, when she'd positioned the boat below him. "Down here!"

Her uncle let go of the spear and dropped heavily into the fishing boat. Balisk lashed the small hull with his tail, splintering a plank of wood. Tom wanted to tackle Sanpao, but the pirate king would have to wait.

"Fight me!" he shouted at the Beast.

Balisk stirred beneath Tom, writhing his muscular body, and reaching with his snapping snake's head.

"Drown him!" ordered Sanpao.

Balisk roared and reared higher out of the water, then plunged beneath the surface. Tom managed to take a deep breath as the water streamed through his clothes and hair. His knuckles were white where he held on with all his strength as Balisk turned over and over, swimming deeper. The water became colder and darker, and the pressure in Tom's ears built until he thought his head might

explode, but still he gripped the fin.
He closed his eyes tight and called
on the power of Sepron's tooth,
the token lodged in his shield. The
burning in his lungs stopped at once
as the magic worked.

Opening his eyes in the stinging
water, he saw the scales the Beast's
body weren't the same all over.
Along the ridge of his back was a
darker strip, the width of Tom's hand,
reaching from head to tail.

Balisk twisted violently and Tom
lost his grip. As Balisk plunged into
the black depths, Tom kicked up
towards the surface. He glimpsed the
black hull of the pirate vessel to his
left. With powerful strokes, he
dragged himself above the waves,
and sucked in deep breaths of air.

Almost at once, he heard Sanpao

snarl and saw the Pirate King leaning over the edge of the ship. Something glinted in his hand, and he hurled it towards Tom.

Tom dived again, and heard the dart thud into the shield on his back. More darts cut into the water around him. One tore through the shoulder

of his tunic, slicing his skin. Tom gritted his teeth as bubbles escaped his mouth, and a trickle of red blood misted off into the water.

I can't give up now! thought Tom, as he headed for the outline of Elenna's fishing craft. He swam beneath it and came up on the other side. "Give me your hand!" he called.

Elenna leaned over and heaved him into the boat. "Thank goodness!" she said. "I thought Sanpao had hit you!"

Her Uncle Leo was sitting on one of the benches, staring fearfully at Sanpao's ship, which drifted some twenty paces away.

"Coward!" bellowed Sanpao. "Wouldn't it be nice if you could call upon some of your belt's special powers, hero of Avantia?"

With a flourish, Sanpao drew aside his tunic. Tom gasped. Around his waist, the Pirate King wore Tom's jewelled belt! Tom's chest tightened with dismay and anger.

"That belongs to me!" shouted Tom. "I won those jewels through fair combat."

"And I stole them through magic!" sneered Sanpao.

Elenna looked at Tom with desperation in her eyes. "Aduro must have given it to him!" she gasped.

Sanpao dropped his hand to the amber jewel. *He's trying to communicate with a Beast!* Tom realised.

"Men, take arms!" Sanpao roared. "It's time to feed these pathetic Avantians to the fish."

CHAPTER NINE

TWIN ENEMIES

The men shouted their approval and lined up along the deck. Others ran from the stern, holding crossbows made from bone. They aimed their strange weapons. Tom glanced into the water, but couldn't see the Beast.

"While there's grog in my veins," said Sanpao, "you'll never take the Tree of Being from me! Men, shoot!" With a succession of thwacking sounds, the air was filled with bolts.

"Duck!" Tom shouted. He grabbed Elenna and her uncle and pushed them down into the boat as the shafts zipped overhead. The iron tip of one bolt punched right through the fishing boat's hull. But the pirates didn't stop at one volley, and a second hail of bolts shot over the boat. Tom risked a look, and saw that the crossbows automatically reloaded, sliding another shaft into the firing mechanism. Sanpao's laughter cut the air above the whizzing barbs.

"You've not seen weapons like this before, have you?" he called.

Elenna strung an arrow and tried to shoot, but she could only lift her head for a moment before ducking for cover again. "There are too many of them!" she gasped. More bolts slammed into the boat.

"Take us closer, helmsman!" bellowed the Pirate King.

The hail of arrows ceased, and Tom dared to lift his head again. Leo's eyes were wide with fear.

We need help, Tom realised, *before Balisk joins the fight again*. Tom touched the scale embedded in his shield, his link to Sepron the Sea Serpent.

As he did so, spray burst from the water beside the fishing boat, showering them all. For a moment Tom dared to hope that Sepron had come already, but he caught a flash of Balisk's silvered scales. The Water Snake lashed his tail like a whip, driving a wall of water at the boat and sending it spinning on the crest of a wave. Tom and the others gripped the sides to stop themselves being thrown out into the waves.

Elenna managed to string an arrow and pointed it at the Beast. Tom saw her eyes narrow. Suddenly the conch shell sounded again.

The Beast launched itself right out of the water, glowing red for a moment. Elenna shot and her shaft whizzed towards Balisk's head, sinking into the scales in its neck.

"Great shot!" he said.

Sanpao laughed as the Beast hovered in mid-air. Tom gasped as its blunt skull seemed to shift beneath its skin, and its head forked in two. As one half of Balisk crashed into the sea, the other split away along the dark stripe down the middle of its body. This piece, with its own head and fins, soared into the air.

"There's two of them!" shouted Elenna. The second Balisk used its fins as wings, propelling it high over Sanpao's ship.

What are we going to do now? Tom asked himself.

"Ready arms!" ordered Sanpao.

The pirates rushed around on deck

to load more bolts into their
crossbows. Tom realised they were
about to face three enemies at once.
The bolts locked into place as the Sea
Balisk hissed from the water and the
Air Balisk began a long swoop
towards them. Tom picked up an oar,
ready to strike it away.

"Get behind me!" he called to the
others.

The pirate ship lurched violently
in the water. The pirates toppled into
each other and the crossbows
clattered to the deck. Two pirates fell
with cries into the water. Only
Sanpao managed to keep his balance.

"What in the name of the High
Seas was that?" he shouted.

A long neck, covered in green
scales, unfurled from the waves,
cascading drops of water. Sepron's

huge, pale eyes flashed with anger, and the sunlight played across the shimmering, rainbow scales.

"Hello, old friend!" Tom yelled.

Sepron opened his mouth and roared back, making the sails on the pirate ship quiver.

"Kill that Beast!" roared Sanpao.

One of the pirates rushed forward with a grappling pole, brandishing it over the deck towards Sepron. The Good Beast closed his jaws, catching the pole and snapping it like a twig.

"Sepron will keep the pirates busy," said Tom. "We need to tackle Balisk."

Elenna was already on her feet, aiming an arrow at the Beast swooping down from the air. Her shaft thudded into one of the horns of its head, making the Beast pull away and hiss with anger. Leo stood with perfect balance on the edge of the boat, stabbing with a fishing spear at the Balisk lurking just beneath the water. The Sea Beast darted away, scales glittering in the sunlight.

Meanwhile, the pirates rushed from one side of the deck to the other, looking for where Sepron might next resurface. Sanpao barked orders, and

none of his attention was on Tom and his friends.

As the Air Beast darted at them again, dodging an arrow, Tom threw his oar aside and drew his sword. In one smooth motion, he managed to slice through one of Air Balisk's horns. The monster hissed in pain, swooping low across the water above its swimming twin. Seeing them so close together gave Tom an idea. If he was going to defeat Balisk, he needed them both in one place. *I can't defeat each of them separately*, he thought. *But I could conquer them together.*

"I have a plan," he said. "Row us over to the sea creature."

"Is that a good idea?" asked Leo.

"Trust me," said Tom.

Elenna and her uncle took the oars and began pulling the vessel towards the Beast. On the pirate ship, Sanpao's crew pushed the crossbow across the deck to shoot at Sepron.

Tom faced the Balisk that hovered in the sky, the rays of sunlight playing on its scales. Tom raised his sword and pointed it at the Beast. "It's me you want. Let's fight!"

The Air Balisk focused on him with both yellow eyes and roared, angling his body into a dive. Tom saw the sea Beast's dark shadow rippling towards them as well. "Get ready to jump out of the boat," Tom hissed to his companions. "I need to bring the two parts of the Beast back together."

The air Beast opened his jaws, flying down. The Sea Balisk disappeared under the boat as Tom saw his own reflection in the flying Balisk's eyes. Now was the time.

"Jump!" he shouted.

He threw himself off the boat with the others. Turning beneath the surface, he saw the Air Balisk smash through the bottom of the boat and collide with its other half. In a flash of red light, the halves began to fuse together.

Tom pulled himself through the water, sword drawn, towards the thrashing Beast. Balisk faced him as the wings disappeared back into his scaly flesh. The two creatures were morphing back into one Beast.

The Sea Balisk lunged and snapped, but Tom smacked the flat of his blade against its nose. The creature jerked away, turning its back on Tom.

Tom aimed his blade carefully, then lunged and buried it deep in the dark stripe that ran down the Beast's back.

A stream of bubbles exploded from Balisk's mouth and nostrils as it twisted round to face Tom. Though Tom knew the Beast could not speak, through the water the creature's eyes spoke of his pain and confusion.

What have you done? the Beast seemed to say. His eyes shone

brighter than ever for a moment, then Tom watched as the light dimmed and fogged over. The Beast's scales cracked and its body dissolved into the water, leaving only empty ocean.

Balisk was no more.

A single claw from one of the Beast's fins floated within reach. Tom snatched it from the water, and tucked it into his animal-hide sash.

Perhaps this token has some power, he thought. Tom was kicking for the surface, already wondering how he would face Sanpao, when he felt a surge from below. He found himself lifted, dripping, out of the water on Sepron's back. Beside him, Elenna supported her terrified uncle.

On the deck of the pirate ship, Sanpao glared at them with hatred.

CHAPTER TEN

A MAGICAL ESCAPE

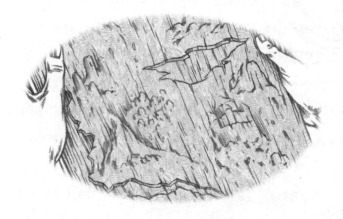

Tom raised his sword and levelled the dripping point at the Pirate King.

"Balisk's defeated," Tom shouted. "Release Aduro, and leave Avantia in peace! It's over, Sanpao."

"Over?" Sanpao bellowed. "My voyage has only just begun! Balisk was my first Beast, and my weakest. He's no more precious to me than a ship's rat! There are five more that will prove a stiffer test for you."

Tom felt a surge of pity for the Beast he'd destroyed, cast aside so easily by a cruel man. "While there's blood in my veins, I'll take on every one of your Beasts!" shouted Tom. He looked to Sepron. Tom pointed his sword towards the ship. "You know what to do," he said.

Sepron raised his massive tail from the water, and brought it crashing down. A huge wave slammed against the side of the pirate vessel, throwing the pirates off balance with a chorus of cries. Sanpao held on.

"Sink them!" shouted Leo.

"Is that all you've got?" Sanpao asked. "Helmsman! Take us away!"

"Again!" shouted Tom.

Sepron drove another wave across

the water. It rocked the pirate ship
again, but something strange was
happening. The vessel seemed to sit
higher out of the water than before.

"It's rising!" gasped Elenna.

The water around the base of the
hull churned into white foam as the
ship rose. More blackened timbers
appeared, coated in barnacles. Tom
stared open-mouthed.

"Unless your Beast has wings,"
roared Sanpao, "it's goodbye – for
now."

The ship lifted clear of the sea, and
water cascaded from the massive
hull. Slowly, the ship turned in the
air. The wind caught in its billowing
sails and Sanpao's vessel climbed
away, disappearing to the north and
into the clouds. Tom and his
companions watched until it was just

a dot near the horizon.

"Sanpao's magic is powerful," said Elenna. "Perhaps he really has bewitched Aduro."

"We should get back on land as quickly as we can," Tom said. "If Sanpao gets there first, he'll hack the tree down."

"We've lost the oars from my boat," said Leo. "What will we do?"

Sepron hissed and turned her head to look at them.

"I think we might have some help," said Tom, smiling.

"I've never travelled so fast!" said Leo, gripping the edge of the fishing boat. "It's like a water chariot!"

Tom and Elenna grinned as the spray soaked their faces. A rope trailed from one of Sepron's fins to the prow of the boat as they shot through the water towards the coast. When they reached the shore, Sepron released them. The boat drifted the rest of the way to land.

Tom, Elenna and Leo jumped out and tugged the boat in, wading up to their ankles in water.

"Thanks, Sepron!" shouted Tom.

The Sea Serpent lashed the water with his tail and gave a roar of farewell. Tom's heart swelled with pride as his Beast friend's shimmering coils sank beneath the waves.

They'd landed some way up the beach from where they'd left Storm, so Tom and Elenna ran along the sand near the water's edge. The stallion whinnied happily to see them. Beyond him, the Tree of Being cast a long shadow across the beach. There was no sign of the pirate vessel. As they walked closer, Tom realised the Tree had changed since the last time they'd been here.

"The trunk looks thicker," he said, stroking the bark. Even the branches seemed more healthy.

"Perhaps it's because we defeated Balisk," said Elenna.

She must be right, Tom thought. Seeing life return to the mighty Tree filled him with hope.

"Maybe when we've vanquished all of Sanpao's Beasts, the Tree will be completely healed," Tom said. "Then the portal might appear to help us rescue my mother and Silver."

"I hope so," said his friend.

The ground shuddered violently beneath their feet. Tom and Elenna gripped each other and Storm reared up, neighing in panic.

"What's happening?" Elenna shouted. The sands shifted around the base of the trunk, collapsing away to reveal the tree's gnarled roots. With a sound of cracking wood, the stunted branches folded down against the tree's trunk, then the central pillar began to sink into the ground. Tom remembered what Aduro had said about the tree moving from place to place.

"It's disappearing!" he gasped.

As the knotted tip of the tree vanished from sight, the sand reformed over the top. Tom walked over. Something was left in the sand.

Tom crouched down and found what looked like a scroll.

"It's bark!" he said, unrolling the

rough parchment.

Elenna stooped at his side. Shapes had been etched onto the surface of the bark, leaving different shades of brown colouring. The reliefs depicted a sketch of the entire Avantian kingdom. It wasn't as detailed as some of the maps Tom had used, but he could feel the powerful magic through his fingertips.

"Look, Tom," said Elenna, pointing to a spot in the Grassy Plains. The small shape of a tree had been scorched into the bark.

"The map must tell us where the Tree will next appear," said Tom.

"But Sanpao might by flying there already," said Elenna.

Tom curled the map up and slotted it into Storm's saddle bag. "No time to lose then." If Tom had any chance of seeing his mother again, he'd have to defeat his most determined and double-crossing enemies yet. *Sanpao is my enemy*, he thought. *And Aduro?* Tom felt sure he was under the Pirate King's thrall. There was nothing for it – no one could save Freya and Silver except Tom and Elenna. They had to return the Tree of Being to full health.

"This isn't going to be easy, is it?" Elenna asked, as they climbed into Storm's saddle.

"Do you want to turn back?" Tom

asked her. He felt a sharp pinch on his back and cried out.

"I came to get you! Remember that girl in the tree? I never turn back."

Tom nodded as he pressed his knees into Storm's sides and the stallion trotted along the beach. "I know," he smiled. "I was just testing."

Elenna waved to her Uncle Leo, who was walking towards them.

"Off so soon?" he shouted. "Perhaps I can give you some dinner?"

"Sorry, Uncle," said Elenna. "Sanpao won't stop. Neither can we."

Her uncle nodded and smiled. "Take care of her, Tom," he said.

Tom grinned. "It's Elenna who looks after me," he said, giving Storm's flanks a nudge. *We'll need each other more than ever this time,* he thought.

KoroN
JAWS
OF DEATH

BY ADAM BLADE

ORCHARD

PROLOGUE

Abraham stepped slowly towards the skittish mare. "There now, Blizzard," he whispered.

The white horse watched him nervously, her eyes rolling, the breath snorting from her nostrils.

Abraham paused, leaning on his staff. He had been working on the Plains as a horse whisperer since boyhood – but this magnificent mare was his most troublesome adversary yet. He could see she had a powerful spirit.

"So, you threw your last rider," he murmured. "And every rider before him, I'll warrant. And you broke down a fence to escape." He clicked his tongue. "That will never do."

The horse bared her teeth, stamping the ground as if she was on the brink of bolting.

"I'll do you no harm," Abraham said, moving forwards again. He was almost upon her now. He reached out an open hand.

Her head dipped and she sniffed his palm, her eyes softening. Abraham came in close, stroking her muscular neck. He lifted the trailing reins.

"That wasn't so bad, was it?" he whispered, getting on to her back. "I'll have you back in the village in no time."

A shadow loomed over them and

Abraham heard a dreadful snarl. The horse's head jerked up, a sharp light igniting in her eyes. She reared on her hind legs, hooves kicking the air, throwing Abraham off. He got up and grabbed her reins, struggling to control her.

He turned and his blood froze as he stared up at a gigantic Beast leaping towards them. It was like a tiger – black as midnight with slashes of blood-red fur across its body – but it was at least three times the size of any tiger he had ever seen.

The great Beast came crashing down a few paces away. Scythe-like claws raked the ground. The fur bristled at the Beast's neck as it drew back its black lips to reveal teeth like daggers. Thick drool dripped from the points of its teeth – hissing and smoking as it scorched the grass.

But even as Abraham tried to understand what he was seeing, his eyes were drawn upwards in horror. Arching high above the monster's back was a thick scorpion-like tail, scaly and tipped with a vicious sting

that dripped green poison.

Abraham scrambled back, not daring to look away. The creature padded forwards, moving slowly, its muscular body rippling. Abraham heard Blizzard snorting and blowing behind him.

The monstrous cat's eyes bored into Abraham. He could hear its harsh breath rasping in its throat, as though its lungs were great bellows.

The Beast roared, jaws gaping. Its stinking breath blasted into Abraham's face. It pounced, rearing high above them and coming down with its claws spread wide and its dripping fangs bared.

Abraham dived aside with a cry of terror. The edge of one massive paw struck him on the shoulder, knocking him to the ground. He watched helplessly as the Beast's claws raked across Blizzard's back, ripping through the flesh. The horse shrieked in pain as she stumbled away.

Abraham staggered to his feet, beating at the tiger-Beast's flanks with his staff. The monster turned, as quick and lithe as any cat, and before Abraham could move, the staff was gripped between its jaws.

Snap! The staff splintered, and now the monster's eyes turned to Abraham.

But even as the Beast's jaws widened to tear apart his body, he saw Blizzard turn her back to the great cat and lash out with her powerful hind legs. The Beast yowled in anger and pain, twisting to face the horse, its sting rising, and pulsing with poison.

"Run!" shouted Abraham. "Run for your life!"

Blizzard whinnied and pounded across the grasslands. With a shivering snarl, the Beast went leaping after her, its high tail lashing.

Abraham gasped for breath as he watched the two creatures race away. He doubted that even such a horse as Blizzard could outrun the fearsome Beast.

Then, a curious whirling, churning sound made him stare upwards. His mouth gaped in astonishment.

"It cannot be!" he gasped.

Sweeping down from the high heavens, its sails billowing and its flag cracking in the wind, was a flying ship!

CHAPTER ONE

THE ENCHANTED WIZARD

Two days had passed since Tom and Elenna had encountered the Pirate King Sanpao and defeated the sea Beast he had set upon them. It had been a fierce battle with a wily and treacherous foe, and Tom worried that worse was to come.

They were riding through the northern reaches of the Forest of

Fear, making for the Grassy Plains and the next stage of their Quest. The air was stifling under the thick branches, and eerie noises came drifting out of the gloomy shadows.

"I wish Silver were with us," said Elenna.

Tom nodded solemnly, knowing how hard it must be for her to be without her noble wolf companion. "We've both lost someone," he said, thinking of his mother, who was also trapped in Tavania. "The only way to free them is to find the Tree of Being."

"That won't be easy," Elenna said angrily. "Not without Aduro."

She was right. The Good Wizard who'd been their friend and guide over so many past Quests was now in thrall to the Pirate King. And Tom's valiant father, Taladon, could not come to their aid either: he lay injured in King Hugo's castle.

Tom's hand moved to his waist, reminding him of something else he had lost. Aduro had stolen his jewelled belt from him and given it to Sanpao, and now the Pirate King controlled the powers of the coloured jewels.

Aduro had used his magic to place a sash of raw animal hide around Tom's waist. Tom had tried to take it off, but it was impossible. Tucked into the sash was a claw that had floated up to him from the Water Beast, Balisk.

"We're on our own," Tom muttered darkly. "Or *almost* on our own. At least we have one thing to guide us."

"The map," Elenna agreed. "Does it

still show the Tree of Being on the Grassy Plains?"

Tom took the scroll of bark from Storm's saddlebag and unrolled it carefully, revealing the finely etched map of Avantia on its surface. A tiny engraved symbol showed that the Tree was still there – but for how long?

The mystical Tree had the power to open portals into other worlds. But it could also move for its own protection, vanishing in an instant into the ground and sprouting up again elsewhere in the Kingdom. It had looked thin and sickly when they had first seen it, but with Balisk defeated, Tom had noticed that the tree seemed a little stronger.

Their Quest was made more urgent and dangerous by the fact that

Sanpao was also seeking the Tree for his own evil purposes. The Pirate King had already damaged it – tearing away one of its branches to use as a mast for his great galleon. If he had control over the entire Tree, Tom knew that his wickedness would have no limits. He would be powerful enough to take over any kingdom he wished – maybe all of them.

"Tom! Look!" Elenna's voice broke into his thoughts. He followed her pointing finger. A pool of eerie blue light was forming among the trees ahead of them.

Tom reined Storm to a halt, sensing dark magic.

His eyes narrowed as the blur of light writhed and twisted and became a vision of their old friend Aduro, staring out at them from his chamber in King Hugo's castle. Tom shivered to see the cruel smile curling Aduro's lip.

"How is your Quest going, my friends?" he asked mockingly.

Tom felt Elenna's hand on his arm, quietly reminding him that Aduro was under an evil spell. Tom knew that the Good Wizard had a true heart, but it was still hard to see him like this.

"It's going very well, thank you," Tom said in a firm voice. "We will never let Sanpao take the Tree of Being. And we will not rest until my mother and Silver are brought safely home!" He raised his chin defiantly. "Tell that to your pirate master!"

Aduro gave a grating laugh. "Foolish boy," he cackled. "Do you not know that King Sanpao is more

mighty than any foe you have faced
before? You'll never see your mother
or that mangy wolf again!"

Tom's anger took over. "I'll never

give up!" he shouted, plucking
Balisk's claw from his sash and
hurling it at the vision. The image
dissolved and the claw scythed
through the blur of blue light, cutting
leaves from the forest trees as it went.

Then, to Tom's astonishment, the

claw curved through the air and came spinning back at him.

He heard Elenna's voice crying out in fear. "Tom! Be careful!"

The claw hissed as it sliced towards his face.

CHAPTER TWO

THE WOUNDED HORSE

Tom ducked and the claw thudded into the trunk of a tree behind them. Elenna let out a gasp of relief.

Tom trotted Storm towards the tree, and tugged the claw free. "This could be a useful weapon," he said.

"I wish my arrows came back to me," Elenna exclaimed.

"All the same, I'm glad Aduro was just a vision," Tom said as he tucked it into his leather sash. "I should never have attacked him like that. We have to remember he is under Sanpao's control!"

Riding on through the day, they came at last to the edge of the forest and found themselves in bright daylight. A fresh breeze wafted over the rolling grasslands that spread before them.

But Storm seemed nervous, as though sensing something was wrong. Tom slipped from the saddle and walked over to a patch of grass.

"What is it?" Elenna asked.

Tom crouched, examining the dark red splashes that stained the ground at his feet. "It's blood," he said. He stood up, pointing out across the

Plain. "A trail of blood."

"What could it be?" Elenna asked anxiously. "A wounded person?"

"Whatever it is, I think we should follow it," Tom said.

Elenna jumped down from the saddle and together they walked through the long grass, Storm following as they tracked the spots of blood.

"Can you hear that?" Tom asked after a while. The sound had been getting gradually louder as they walked. *Running water.*

They found themselves in a wide valley, gazing down at a slender silver stream that went dancing over a bed of brown stones.

"I think we've found the wounded animal," Tom said softly.

A white mare stood fetlock deep in

the flowing water, her head lowered
to drink. She was saddled and her
reins dangled in the water, but there
was no sign of a rider. Four parallel
wounds ran in a ragged line down the
creature's side, and even as she drank,
her blood dripped into the water.

Tom scanned the horizon for

any sign of danger.

"Stay back," said Elenna. "We mustn't frighten her. Let me go first."

Elenna made her way down towards the horse.

The mare's head rose suddenly and she turned, ears laid back, tail flicking nervously. Tom held his breath. Would the animal bolt? But even at this distance, he could see the light of intelligence in the horse's eyes.

"Oh, you poor thing," Tom heard Elenna say. "Trust me – we'll make you better."

The mare shivered, tossing her mane and shaking her head. But she didn't bolt, and a few moments later, Elenna had the reins in her hands as she stroked the horse's muzzle.

"It's all right," she called to Tom. "You can come now."

As he approached the beautiful animal, Tom could see how badly she had been hurt. Dried blood encrusted the four deep gashes.

"Only a Beast could do that," he muttered. *But what kind of Beast?* he wondered.

Taking the talon of Epos the Flame Bird from the face of his shield, he very gently touched it to the first of the wounds. The mare whinnied and shied away, but Elenna held her steady. Tom ran the talon along the cut, then moved quickly to the next one. Even as he worked on the second wound, he saw the raw lips of torn flesh closing up, mending so completely that in a few moments there was not even a scar or a mark on the horse's white hide.

Tom healed the final wounds, and

the mare's eyes filled with gratitude and relief.

"There," Tom said. "All better." But then something caught his attention. There was another injury, high on the horse's back, behind the saddle. It was different from the long gouges – a painful-looking brand burned into the white hide.

"Sanpao!" Tom hissed angrily, instantly recognising the evil shape of the brand. It was a Beast skull with horns – the mark of the Pirate King.

"The Pirates did this?" Elenna gasped. "Are they here already?"

"They must be," exclaimed Tom. He snatched out the map, his finger following the route they had taken from the forest to the stream. If the map was accurate, then the Tree of

Being was close by – only a short gallop away.

"We may still be in time!" he said, running to Storm and leaping into the saddle. "Elenna – stay with the horse. I have to find the Tree!"

He urged Storm into a canter up the long grassy slope. There was no time to lose! He couldn't let the pirates reach the Tree of Being first.

As he approached the crest of the hill, he heard the thud of hooves behind. He turned his head, surprised to see Elenna riding the white horse, and catching up fast.

Side by side, they came to the hilltop. The undulating plain stretched away to the far horizon.

"We should be able to see the Tree now!" Tom shouted, staring desperately out over the grasslands.

He pointed to a hollow at the foot of the hill. "It should be right there!"

"I don't understand," said Elenna.

Tom turned grimly to her. "I think I know what this means," he growled. "Sanpao has already been here – he's taken the Tree!" Anger and frustration boiled up in him. "It means we've failed."

CHAPTER THREE
DIRTY TRICKS

"Who's that?" Elenna was pointing along the ridge of the hill. A man stood there, dressed in peasant clothes and waving at them.

"He may have seen what happened," said Tom as they rode along the ridge.

"You found her, thank goodness!" said the man, nodding to the horse as they came to a halt in front of him.

"Her name is Blizzard, and mine is Abraham. I've been searching for her." He frowned, obviously puzzled. "But she was wounded: the claw-marks…?"

"There's no time to explain," Tom said, spotting a curious, unsettling light in the man's eyes. He had seen it somewhere before – but where? "Have you seen anything unusual on the Plains?" he asked.

"I have seen horrors and nightmares in my homeland," Abraham replied with a grimace. "I was attacked by a Beast." His eyes widened. "But then I saw something impossible. A flying ship! A great galleon with a crew of men bearing strange curved swords."

"We've met them before," growled Tom. "They're pirates, and their leader is a man named Sanpao. Did you see where they went?"

"Their ship made for my homestead," said Abraham. "I fear they'll plunder my house and steal my horses."

"Is it far?" asked Tom.

"At the gallop, we could be there very quickly," said Abraham.

"Elenna," said Tom. "Climb up behind me on Storm – let Abraham ride Blizzard." He turned to the man. "Take us to your home."

They'd only been galloping over the plain for a short while when Tom saw an isolated farmstead in front of them. There was a house and a barn, and several paddocks with high fences and strong wooden gates.

But the paddock gates were open and there was no sign of any horses.

Reining Blizzard up, Abraham slipped down from the saddle, falling to his knees, with his fists raised in despair. "They have already been here!" he cried. "All my horses have been taken!"

Tom and Elenna dismounted. Elenna looked into Tom's eyes and he knew exactly what she was thinking. *Too late, again!*

Abraham staggered to his feet and stumbled into one of the enclosures. "All is lost!" he cried. "I'm ruined!"

Tom and Elenna followed him into the corral.

"You're alive, and that's something," Elenna told him. "The Beast or the pirates might have killed you!"

The man turned, his eyes burning. "They might," he exclaimed. "But they didn't!" And with that, he ran past them, sending them both spinning. Tom knew that something was wrong – but before he could even draw his sword, Abraham had dashed through the gate and had swung it closed behind them. The iron bolt clanged as he threw it across.

"You tricked us!" Tom raged, hurling himself at the gate. He could see Abraham's gleaming eyes through gaps in the planking. Now he knew where he had seen that strange light before. In the eyes of Aduro!

"Let us out," shouted Elenna.

"It's useless talking to him," Tom spat. "He's under Sanpao's spell!"

Outside the corral, Storm neighed loudly.

"You won't keep us locked up here for long!" Tom shouted to Abraham. He began to climb the gate, with

Elenna only a fraction behind him.

"I don't need to," Abraham cried.
"Can't you hear? They're coming!"

Tom reached the top of the gate as
a dreadful sight met his eyes. A great
band of pirates – a score or more –
galloped in from all sides, their
ponytails floating out behind them.
As they raised their curved swords
high, they howled ferocious war-cries.

The two friends climbed over the gate and jumped down on the other side. Abraham was watching the pirates with a triumphant grin on his face. The horses the pirates were riding must have come from the empty corral, Tom realised.

"Stay close to me," he warned Elenna as he drew his sword and lifted his shield. "We have to make

a run for Storm. We may still be able to ride between them."

Elenna had an arrow to her bow as the two of them sped towards the waiting horse.

The pirates drew up sharply, their eyes flashing and their swords bright and cruel in the sunlight. They had the farmstead surrounded. To get past them, Tom and Elenna would have to battle for their lives.

But even as they neared Storm, a deep shadow loomed over them and a voice boomed out from above: "Stop!"

Tom looked up as the Pirate King's galleon came racing across the sky, like a great flying castle, fortified with turrets and battlements. Its blood red sails billowed, the Beast skull flag snapping in the wind. As Tom gazed

up at the dreadful sight, he saw the
Pirate King himself staring down at
them.

"We meet again!" Sanpao called.
"Trust me – this time will be the last!"

CHAPTER FOUR

BETRAYED BY A FRIEND

The terrible pirate ship came thundering down, crushing the wooden walls of the paddocks with its slimy, barnacled hull. The vessel's sails rippled and its timbers groaned as it came to a halt, looming over the farmstead like a hideous mountain of wood, canvas and iron.

Tom and Elenna sprang back as a

gangplank was pushed down. Storm
and Blizzard whinnied in alarm, and
Abraham was on his knees with his
arms spread in greeting. The Pirate
King appeared at the ship's rail.

"My master!" Abraham whined.
Tom's fist tightened around his sword
hilt, and at his side he saw that
Elenna was ready with her bow.

But they were surrounded. How

could they hope to win a fight against so many? "Don't shoot him," Tom murmured to Elenna. "Let's wait for a better chance to escape."

Tom eyed the Pirate King with contempt as he came stamping down the gangplank. The skin on Sanpao's face and neck and arms was stained with dark tattoos and his long ponytail hung down his back, studded with sharp iron darts.

A vicious grin stretched across Sanpao's scarred face. His cutlass was sheathed, and he carried a huge double-headed axe across his powerful shoulders.

He's still wearing my belt! Tom thought angrily, seeing the jewels glinting at the Pirate King's waist.

Sanpao towered over Tom and Elenna. All around them, the

mounted pirates roared. "Greetings to our great King! Greetings to Sanpao the unconquerable!"

"How shall I reward your insolence, boy?" he growled. "Should I slice your head clean off your shoulders? Or something more amusing? Cut your body into small pieces for the entertainment of my crew?"

Tom stared steadily into his face. As before, he noticed how the pirate's left eye was half closed, the lid pressed down by thick scar tissue.

"Do your worst!" said Tom. "I'm not afraid of you."

Tom scanned the vessel quickly and his spirits lifted a little. There was no sign of the Tree of Being on the ship. Blizzard snorted and skittered backwards.

"There she is," said Sanpao. "We branded the nag, but she escaped again."

"Maybe she can smell evil," hissed Elenna.

"Listen to her!" howled one of the pirates. "Kill them, sire! Cut them into chops! Boil their bones and feed 'em to the dogs!"

"You should have stayed away from me, boy," spat Sanpao. "You and your feisty friend. Ha! See how she glares at me! Would you like to fire an arrow at me, missy? You'd be dead before it struck!"

"It might be worth it to rid the world of you!" snarled Elenna, raising her bow and aiming an arrow straight at the Pirate King's heart.

"Brave words, girl!" laughed Sanpao.

"Lower your bow, Elenna," Tom

whispered. "This isn't the way."

"Wisely said," said Sanpao. "But empty your mind of any thoughts of escape. You will die, and how you behave will dictate whether your deaths are swift or prolonged. But in the meantime, I have other duties to attend to." He bared his teeth in a fierce grin. "My pet wizard has told me that the Tree of Being will appear near here very soon." He raised a clenched fist. "I will take its power for my own, and there is nothing you two can do to stop me!"

Anger and hatred welled up in Tom. Yelling with rage, he flung himself at the Pirate King, hoping desperately to deliver a killing blow before he was cut down.

Sanpao stepped neatly aside. The great battleaxe was off his shoulder

in an instant, sweeping through the
air and striking against Tom's shield.
Tom swung his sword. It rang against
the axe, but he was allowed only one
blow before the Sanpao thrust his
axe-head forward into Tom's chest,
knocking him over.

Undaunted, Tom leaped to his feet,
ready to attack again.

"Tom! Watch out!" Elenna cried,
and at the same moment Tom saw
Storm springing forward from where

he had been standing at Blizzard's side. For a moment, he thought the noble horse was coming to his aid, but suddenly the stallion turned and let fly with his back legs.

Stunned, Tom only just had time to bring his shield up to block the kick. Storm's hooves struck against his shield, hurling him backwards so that he fell and rolled helplessly almost to the Pirate King's feet.

"Storm! No!" shouted Elenna.

But her voice was drowned by the hideous cheering of the pirates and by Sanpao's bellowing laughter.

Tom's mind was still reeling. What had happened? Had the loyal animal struck out blindly, thinking he was aiming for the Pirate King?

Sanpao called out. "To me, my faithful steed! Come to your master!"

Storm trotted obediently to Sanpao, and now Tom could see the eerie light that gleamed in the animal's eyes. *Just like Abraham and Aduro!*

The Pirate King swung himself up into the saddle, dragging back on the reins and digging his heels cruelly into Storm's flanks. The horse reared and neighed, foam flying from his lips.

Sanpao glared down at him. "You see, boy? There is nothing of yours that I cannot take. Nothing!"

As Tom lay in the dirt and saw the pirate's evil spell flickering in Storm's eyes, he began to fear that Sanpao may be right. But the doubts only troubled him for an instant. The next moment he was up on his feet, sword ready, his shield steady on his arm. Even if this Quest were to be the death of him – he would not give up.

CHAPTER FIVE

THE SHIP
OF DEATH

As Tom rushed at the Pirate King,
Sanpao forced Storm to rear up and
lash out with his hooves. Tom moved
in, dodging to avoid the thrashing
hooves and the long swings of
Sanpao's axe. If he could just manage
one good thrust with his sword!

But the amber jewel of the
mammoth, Tusk, was glowing at

Sanpao's waist, boosting his battle skills, and Tom was unable to get past his guard.

He's using my own powers against me! thought Tom. *I'll make him pay for that.*

Storm's flailing hoof crashed against Tom's shield, driving him to his knees. As he fought to get to his feet again, the axe struck Tom's sword from his hand, sending it spinning through the air. Sanpao jumped down from the saddle and ripped Tom's shield from his arm, bringing the blade of his axe to a halt a hair's breadth from Tom's neck.

Panting, Tom stared up at Sanpao.

"Enough of this!" shouted the Pirate King. He stared up at his ship. "Kimal! My first mate – I leave you in charge. Do what you will with these weak *children*! I must go and

await the coming of the Tree!"

Sanpao tossed Tom's shield away and sprung onto Storm's back. He wrenched on the reins and then turned and galloped off, heading towards the hollow under the hill, where the Tree of Being was to appear.

Elenna had already been grabbed by pirates and her bow and quiver of arrows had been torn from her. The pirates hauled Tom to his feet. He felt disheartened and ashamed to have failed so completely. The Pirate King had his belt *and* his horse.

And it won't be long before he has the Tree of Being, thought Tom.

Tom struggled as the pirates tied ropes around him, but there were too many of them and soon his arms were pinned helplessly to his sides.

"You cowards!" shouted Elenna. "Give us our weapons and fight us one-to-one!" But the pirates just laughed at her as they knotted more ropes around their ankles. Tom couldn't do a thing as the pirates lifted them shoulder-high and carried them up the gangplank to the ship.

Tom strained against the ropes as the pirates threw the two friends down onto the deck. He winced in pain as he struck the boards, and he heard Elenna groan. Fortunately, they were close together and facing one another. Tom looked into Elenna's eyes, seeing fear in them. A trickle of blood ran from her lip.

"We'll think of something, don't worry," Tom whispered. His words were cut off by a kick in the back.

"Be quiet, you rats!"

Tom stared up at the first mate. Kimal was a huge brute, his bare chest crisscrossed with scars, his skull patterned with evil-looking tattoos.

"Release me and give me my sword, and you'll soon see how this rat fights back!" Tom snarled.

Kimal threw back his head and laughed. "You'll beg for a swift death by the time we are done with you," he said. "But first things first." He turned, shouting to his crew. "Bring the horses aboard."

The timbers of the pirate ship boomed as the mounted pirates came pounding aboard. As the gangplank was drawn up, Tom noticed that Blizzard was not among the horses. The fierce mare must have proved too hard to handle.

Good for her! Tom thought.

Kimal took Tom and Elenna by the scruff of their necks and dragged them to their feet. He brought them to the ship's rail as the red sails filled and the ship shuddered in preparation for flight.

"Tie them to the gunwales," Kimal ordered. Two pirates came forwards and bound Tom and Elenna's feet to the ship's rail. Then, with its sails stretching and its ropes humming, the huge galleon rose into the air.

"Where are you taking us?" Elenna demanded.

"Would you like a better view?" Kimal asked. "I think that can be arranged." He grasped each of them in one of his massive fists and lifted them off the ground.

Shaking with laughter, he heaved them over the rail.

Tom's legs thrashed in the air as he stared down. The ground shrank away, far below. For a moment he hung there at Elenna's side, his feet dangling, and then, to his horror, Kimal let go. They plunged downwards. Tom's ears were filled with the hissing of the wind, and his stomach turned over and over.

Half-way to the ground, the ropes pulled them up sharply, biting into Tom's ankles, jarring his body, and making him cry out in agony. Elenna hung at his side, upside down. Laughter drifted down from the ship. Tom twisted his head and saw the faces of the pirates staring down at them as they swung helplessly in the wind. He saw one of them hurl something. It was a knife. It sliced the air close to the taut rope.

So that was the plan! The pirates were playing a vicious game with them – and the sport would only end when the two of them were sent tumbling helplessly to their deaths.

"Again!" shouted Kimal. "A golden coin to the man who cuts them loose!"

CHAPTER SIX

SKULLS AND HOOVES

Tom felt dizzy and disorientated as he twisted at the end of the long rope. More knives spun past and the pirates yelled and cheered. It would only be a matter of time before one of the knives struck home and the ropes were cut.

And then I will never find the Tree of Being, he thought desperately.

My mother and Silver will be trapped for all time!

The pirate ship cleaved through the sky, passing over dense forests and rocky outcrops. Tom ground his teeth in frustration, the blood thundering in his head, the ropes cutting into his flesh. All the time, the Tree of Being was getting further away. But then he saw that their flight was taking them towards a great lake that stretched out to the north of the Plains.

An idea formed in his mind. He strained against the ropes that bound his arms to his sides. They loosened a fraction and he was able to worm his hand up to his chest. His fingers closed around the claw in his sash and he cautiously edged it out.

"Don't drop it," warned Elenna, watching him intently and

understanding what he was trying to do.

He began to saw at his bonds.

One by one the strands of rope came free. They were almost over the water now and he was unbound save for the ropes around his ankles. So far the pirates hadn't noticed what Tom was doing. He could hear them shouting at one another; they were busy making wagers on who would win Kimal's gold coin. A thrown knife slashed dangerously close to his face and another tore a slice from Elenna's sleeve.

"Ha!" roared a pirate. "The gold coin is almost mine!"

Tom finally split the ropes on his wrists and shook his hands free. Kimal's voice rose above the others. "The boy is cutting through the ropes! Kill them! Kill them both, now!"

Tom had to act quickly. He swung himself towards Elenna and caught hold of her, sawing at the ropes around her chest. He could hear the pirates shouting and howling. More knives came hurtling down. The pirates were no longer aiming at the ropes – their targets were Tom and Elenna's dangling bodies.

Tom saw the waters of the lake glistening below them now.

"Trust me!" he gasped as he cut the rope around Elenna's feet.

"Always!"

She fell, lifting her arms over her head as she scythed down into the water. A moment later Tom sawed through his own rope and plunged after her.

The water was freezing. Bubbles filled Tom's vision as he sank deeper and deeper. He twisted in the darkness, striking upwards, his lungs aching for air, his head pounding.

He broke the surface with a gasp, still clutching the claw in his fist, treading water as he turned his head this way and that in search of Elenna. Where was she? Had she drowned?

"Elenna!" he called frantically.

There was a rush of water close by him and his friend's head appeared.

"I'm all right!" she panted, her hair sticking to her face, and a defiant gleam in her eyes.

Tom pushed the claw back into his sash and, keeping close together, they swam for the shore. Tom looked up as they clambered out of the lake.

The pirate ship had turned and the crew were busy on deck with some large object that they were hauling to the rail.

"What is that?" Elenna asked. "It's not the bone crossbow they used before."

"I think it's a catapult," Tom said. "They're loading it! We have to run!"

He saw the pirates place a white object on the firing arm of the weapon. A moment later the catapult released with a sharp snapping sound. The white object came spinning towards them.

It was a human skull! Tom pushed Elenna to one side then dived in the opposite direction as the horrible missile crashed into the ground and exploded into fragments of bone.

Tom scrambled to his feet, pulling

Elenna up in her dripping clothes.

Another skull shot down at them, landing with a splash in the shallow water.

"Run!" Tom shouted.

They raced over the uneven

ground, zigzagging to avoid being easy targets. All the while, the ship loomed nearer, casting its massive shadow across the ground.

"Run them down!" bellowed Kimal.

Tom heard a whistle beside his head as one of the skulls thumped into the ground beside him. "They're getting closer!" he called to Elenna.

They leaped over a ditch, and Tom grabbed Elenna's arm, veering aside along the length of the channel.

"Bring us about!" shouted Sanpao's first mate. The ship creaked and the sails snapped with the sudden manoeuvre. Tom had bought them some time. He and Elenna charged and stumbled over the uneven ground, until suddenly he heard hooves. The ground began to shake under his feet, as though a thousand cattle were stampeding towards them.

"It's Tagus!" shouted Elenna as the huge Beast came galloping into view. His man's chest heaved and his horse's flanks glistened with sweat as he came pounding towards them, lifting one powerful arm in greeting.

Glad as he was to see the Good Beast, Tom had a sense of foreboding

as he remembered that Sanpao commanded evil Beasts of his own. How long would it be before the Pirate King unleashed one of his fearsome Beasts on them?

"Tagus came without being summoned!" Tom cried. Never in his life had he been so pleased to meet an old friend. The ship was coming straight for them, and Kimal gripped the deck-rail, his face set in a scowl.

"He must have seen the ship," Elenna said. "Thank you, Tagus!"

Tagus came to a halt, growling in greeting as they clambered up on to his back. But the ship was so close now that Tom could smell the rotting filth that caked its hull.

The pirates sent another skull missile hurtling down. It burst into bony shards close by Tagus's front hoof.

"Go!" Tom shouted, digging his heels into the Beast's broad flanks. He leaned forwards, pointing back the way they'd come. "That way, Tagus!"

Although the Beast didn't understand human speech, he understood what Tom wanted. Tom and Elenna clung on desperately as Tagus took off at a gallop.

Tom looked up. The pirate ship was close behind, its sails straining as it raced after them.

"Run while you can!" Kimal cried. "You won't escape us! We'll pursue you to the ends of the world!"

Even as the dreadful threat echoed in Tom's ears, he saw a skull speeding directly towards him. He was unarmed and his shield was gone. He had no hope of avoiding the deadly missile!

CHAPTER SEVEN

THE BEAST COMES

Tagus twisted to one side at the very last moment. The skull grazed past Tom's shoulder and broke into jagged fragments in the grass. But the ship was gaining at an alarming speed. It's terrible shadow swept over them as it cleaved through the air.

Tom leaned forward, shouting at the top of his voice. "Tagus! You have to run quicker!"

The Horse-Man gave a snort, his brawny arms pumping the air. Tom hung on grimly to the Good Beast's waist as Tagus put on a sudden spurt of speed. Elenna's hands gripped his waist.

"We should retrieve our weapons," he heard her shout against the wind of their wild gallop.

"Go that way, Tagus!" Tom shouted, pointing. The Beast nodded and veered to one side, and it was all Tom could do to stay on his back as he went careering over the plain towards Abraham's farmstead.

Tom risked a look over his shoulder. The pirate ship was falling behind now, and he could see Kimal roaring in frustration as he swung the wheel to try and keep up with them. They reached the farmstead

and Tom shouted for Tagus to pull
up. The Good Beast halted so
suddenly that Tom was almost hurled
into the grass. The Horse-Man's chest
and flanks rose and fell as he caught
his breath, and there was a fierce

smile on his face as Tom and Elenna jumped down and searched for their weapons.

Tom found his shield and sword, and Elenna her bow and quiver just beside the shattered corral. Tom glanced up at the sky, seeing the pirate ship closing in on them again.

Elenna notched an arrow to the string and pulled it back, her knuckles whitening on the bow. Her arms trembled a little as she held it taut. She closed one eye, aiming along the shaft of the arrow, holding her breath. The bow steadied in her hands, then she shot.

The shaft sped swift and true up towards the ship. It struck Kimal in the shoulder. He staggered back, bellowing in pain, and losing his grip on the wheel. The great hoop of wood spun out of control and the pirate ship sheered away, twisting to one side and tipping forwards so that the crew fell about the decks.

"Great shot!" Tom declared, smiling at Elenna.

"I hope so," Elenna replied, watching anxiously as the doomed ship plunged towards the ground.

Kimal lunged at the wheel, grasping it in both hands to hold it steady. The prow of the great ship lifted and the decks began to level. But not enough.

With an impact that shook the ground, the keel ploughed into the grass with a deafening crash, churning up huge clods of earth. The ship came to a grinding halt.

To Tom's dismay, he saw that it was undamaged. But there was panic aboard as the newly captured horses broke free and began to gallop across the deck and leap over the gunwales to freedom.

"I don't think they'll be bothering

us for a while," Tom said with grim satisfaction as he saw Kimal trying vainly to muster his men. "Now we can face Sanpao!"

Elenna and Tom sprang up on to Tagus's back again. As though the Beast knew what was needed from him, he broke into a gallop – and this time he was heading straight for the place where the Tree of Being should have appeared.

"It's already there!" cried Tom as they rode up the hill. The Tree was unmistakeable. It soared into the sky, towering over the Plains, taller than any tree Tom had ever seen. Tom could see that it was no longer dying. The branches, though still bare, stood out more proudly from the trunk, and there were fewer patches of disease on the bark.

But as they came to the crest of the hill, he saw that the tree was in deadly peril.

Sanpao stood at its base, the double-headed battleaxe in his hands. And Abraham was with him, wielding a smaller axe.

"They're going to chop the tree down!' cried Elenna.

Worst of all, Storm stood quietly to one side with Blizzard, both horses still trapped in the Pirate King's thrall, their eyes glowing eerily.

"Sanpao!" Tom shouted. "Stop!"

At his back, Elenna levelled an arrow as Tagus cantered down the hill towards the two men.

Sanpao rested his axe on his shoulder, watching them approach. If he was surprised or alarmed at the sight of the Good Beast, he didn't show it. A grin spread across his scarred face.

The Pirate King drew in a deep breath and let out a shout. "Koron!"

"What's Koron?" Elenna asked.

Tom pointed to a creature that was approaching them at great speed across the Plains. "He is, I think!" he said.

The massive, tiger-like Beast had black fur streaked with ugly red markings, and stiff hairs bristled like wire around his neck. The loathsome yellow slits of his eyes burned with malice, and his black lips were drawn back from drooling fangs. Where his thick spittle hit the grass, it left smoking scorch marks. Great claws gouged the ground as he bounded towards the Tree, roaring ferociously. A scaly, curving tail lifted over the fearsome Beast's back, ending in a terrible sting that glistened with green venom.

Tom drew his sword, preparing for the fight of his life. But Koron was not heading for them – he bounded towards the Pirate King. Hope grew in Tom's heart. Despite his monstrous appearance, might Koron be a Good Beast? Might he attack Sanpao?

The Pirate King was still staring up at Tagus and the two friends, almost as if he was unaware of the huge Beast bearing down on him. But then, at the last possible moment, Sanpao turned, flexing his knees and spreading his arms.

Tom watched in amazement as the Pirate King leaped into the air. He back-flipped with supple strength over the Beast's head, and landed easily astride the monster's shoulders.

Sanpao brandished his axe. "Dare you face me now, boy?" he shouted. "Dare you face Koron, Jaws of Death?"

CHAPTER EIGHT

THE BLINDING VENOM

Tom lifted his sword high. "I don't fear you or your Beast!" he shouted to the Pirate King. He turned quickly to Elenna. "Jump down," he said. "Make sure Abraham can't do any harm to the Tree with that axe of his. Tagus and I will deal with Sanpao!"

"Be careful!" Elenna said as she dropped from the Good Beast's back.

"Sanpao is dangerous enough on his *own*."

Tom narrowed his eyes as he turned back to his enemies. "Tagus! Take me to them!" he called. "Let's show them how we fight!"

Koron turned now and came pounding up the hill towards Tom and his friends. The Beast's slavering mouth gaped wide, spitting deadly drool, the yellow fangs bared like great curved daggers. And as he ran, the scaly tail lashed from side to side above his back, spraying vile green venom.

Tagus reared up with a roar, and careered down the hillside towards Koron and the Pirate King. Tom clung onto the Beast's wide back, and lifted his shield.

I have to defeat Sanpao and his Beast, Tom thought grimly. *If the Tree of*

Being is destroyed, I may never see my mother again.

Sanpao let out a shrill cry as Koron loped up the hillside.

"Attack!" shouted Tom, as the four enemies rushed at one another. "For Freya and for Silver!"

Neither Beast veered off as they came together. Tagus reared up on his strong horse legs, his fore-hooves striking the air. Koron's hairy pelt gave off a sickening, overpowering stench that filled Tom's head and made it hard to concentrate. The evil Beast's jaws snapped, spitting the venomous drool. Sanpao's reach was longer than Tom's and as the Pirate King swung his great axe, Tom had to duck aside to avoid being cut in two. The Beasts grazed past one another, Tagus striking out with his fists and Koron's fangs

gnashing, while above them the vicious tail lunged and stabbed.

Tom saw that Koron was aiming his sting at Tagus's face. But the mighty Horse-Man swung his arm and beat the tail aside with a bellow of anger. Tagus was a fearsome fighter, but Tom wondered how long he could survive against the speed and viciousness of Sanpao's Beast.

Sanpao swung the axe again. This

time it clanged against Tom's shield, almost sending him reeling from Tagus's back. But he gripped on tightly with his legs and managed to regain his balance. The two Beasts turned and came together a second time, Tagus roaring in anger, and Koron hissing and spraying thick spittle from his mouth.

This battle was like the jousts that Tom had watched in King Hugo's palace – except that this was no honourable sport and Tom knew only too well that Sanpao wouldn't hesitate to kill him.

Tagus drew back, his teeth bared, his fists pumping the air, breathing hard as he watched the evil Beast's tail swaying above Sanpao's head.

Koron's head dropped, his drool burning the grass. His eyes were on the Good Beast, filled with evil fury. Through the black and red fur, Tom could see the muscles of the Beast's huge body tensing as Koron prepared to spring. On the Beast's back, Sanpao was grinning savagely, as though he knew the battle was already won. Tom stared into Sanpao's face, trying to think of a way to get within striking distance of the Pirate King without falling victim to his huge axe.

The talon of Balisk!

Tom suddenly remembered his new weapon. He sheathed his sword and snatched the claw from his sash, flinging it at Sanpao with all his might. Sanpao jerked to one side, but the claw cut a deep wound high on his right arm. Blood sprayed as the Pirate King howled with pain. The axe fell from his grip, and he rocked sideways on his Beast's back.

A look of absolute rage came over his face as he lost balance and fell, thudding heavily into the long grass.

His heart hammering in his chest, Tom raised his hand to snatch the claw as it came spinning back to him. But as he closed his fingers about it, the claw exploded into fine dust. Tom gave a gasp of dismay. *What had happened?*

He heard the Pirate King roar with laughter. "Did you not know?" he jeered. "The tokens from these Beasts can only be used once! You must fight Koron with nothing but your sword and shield. And they will be little protection for you!"

No sooner had the words left Sanpao's mouth than Koron leaped at Tom and the terrible sting lashed down. Tom lifted his shield to block the blow, feeling the barbed sting strike off the wood, almost unseating him with its force.

Tom sliced with his sword, hoping

to sever the sting. But Koron
bounded to one side before the sword
could bite, his jaws gaping wide and
spraying saliva into Tagus's face.

Tagus let out a bellow of agony.
Tom saw smoke rising up from
between Tagus's fingers. Patches
of the Good Beast's hair had been
scorched away, leaving raw wounds.

Howling in pain, the blinded Beast
stumbled away across the hillside, his
legs buckling, his hands clutching at
his sightless eyes. Tagus tripped on
a jutting rock and fell heavily onto
his side. Tom was thrown off and
went rolling down the hill.

Coming to a breathless halt, he felt
the ground vibrating under him. He
stared up and saw Koron pounding
through the air towards him, claws
bared and sting poised.

CHAPTER NINE

THE POISONED STING

Tom thrust his shield up, drawing in his head and limbs so that the burning spittle couldn't splash his skin. The face of his shield smoked, but the wood was too powerful to be affected by Koron's saliva. Tom had learned on his battle with Balisk that it was made from the Tree of Being.

The power of the Tree is stronger than

Koron's acid! Tom thought. *At least that's something to be grateful for.*

With a speed and agility honed by countless fights, Tom jumped quickly to his feet again, his sword poised and his shield at the ready.

A guttural laugh made him glance to the side. "Come, Horse-Man!" mocked the Pirate King, standing near the fallen Tagus with his fists on his hips. "Look me in the eyes and you shall see the man who will be your master!"

The blinded Beast struggled vainly to get up, his hands over his eyes, his flesh smouldering.

"That will never happen!" Tom shouted, catching a glimpse of the pitiful wounds on the Good Beast's face. "Tagus will never be your slave!"

Tom wanted desperately to go to his old friend's aid – but there was no time. Koron was crouched low, staring at Tom with raging eyes, the fur around his neck bristling and his sting swaying from side to side.

Sanpao laughed again and pointed to Koron. "All Beasts must do my bidding!"

"But not all *people!*" Tom heard Elenna shout from near the Tree, where she was guarding Abraham with an arrow on the bow-string. "You can beat them both, Tom! I know you can!"

Heartened by Elenna's encouragement, Tom squared up to the Beast, thrusting all other thoughts from his mind.

Koron's lips drew back from his knife-like fangs and his jaws opened in a long, vicious growl. The great claws sank into the ground. Tom spread his legs for better balance, his eyes fixed on the Beast.

Koron sprang, all claws and fangs. Quick as lightning, Tom leaped aside, lunging at the Beast's throat with his sword then darting out of reach of the stabbing sting. The venomous point slashed down a hair's-breadth from his shoulder, spraying poison.

Koron twisted and attacked again. The claws raked down Tom's shield, but again he managed to sidestep and stabbed once more at the Beast's throat. But Koron was too quick to be caught like that. Instead the flat of Tom's blade struck hard against the Beast's muzzle.

Koron retreated a few steps, snarling furiously, shaking his head in pain.

"That's to pay you back for the pain you caused Blizzard!" Tom shouted as he hurled himself forwards and leaped onto the Beast's back. He straddled the hairy neck just as he had seen Sanpao do. If he could stay mounted like this on the Beast, he had the chance to thrust his sword in deep and destroy Koron with one blow.

Koron bucked and thrashed as he tried to throw off his unwanted rider. Tom grasped tufts of fur in each hand, using all his strength just to stay on the crazed Beast. Thrown back and forth and side to side, he could feel every bone in his body being shaken loose and his teeth rattling in his skull.

The angry Beast yowled and spat as it fought to cast Tom off. An instinct made Tom turn and lift his shield. Just in time! He had almost forgotten the whipping tail.

The sting jabbed down, hammering onto the shield and spraying venom. Tom swung his blade over his shield, hoping to sever the sting from the tail. But Koron's tail snapped to the side, striking against his sword and sending it spinning from Tom's hand.

Tom's heart faltered as he clung to the Beast's thick fur. He was unarmed now, and the only protection he had was his shield. Again and again the tail came plunging down. Each time, Tom managed to fend it off. But how long could this go on? How long before Koron managed to throw him off or find a way through his defences?

"Kill him!" Tom heard Sanpao's

voice above the snarls of the Beast. "Mighty Koron! Hurl him off! Rend him with your claws! Break his bones with your teeth! Poison his blood with your sting!"

Cold anger filled Tom – and with the anger came an idea. He had no weapons with which to attack the Beast – but Koron's own weapon might be made to work in his favour.

He twisted, staring upwards, waiting for the tail to lash down again.

He needed to time this perfectly.

Holding his breath, he saw the sting descending. At the last possible moment, he flung himself from the Beast's back. As he had hoped, the unstoppable power of the tail sent the venomous point of the sting deep into Koron's neck.

Tom landed in the grass, rolling over, winded and dizzy. He heard the evil Beast shriek and howl.

"No!" Sanpao bellowed.

Tom climbed to his feet. His plan had worked! Koron was writhing, straining his head around as though trying to bite at the sting embedded in his neck. Strange snarling sounds came from the Beast's flexing jaws.

Suddenly Koron shuddered and slumped to the ground. His black hair faded to a dull grey, and the huge flanks twitched as the legs kicked feebly. The Beast let out a final miserable whine and, as Tom watched in astonishment, Koron dissolved into a mist of fine grey ash that drifted away on the breeze.

The Beast was gone!

CHAPTER TEN

TO FIGHT ANOTHER DAY

"You'll pay for destroying my Beast!" shouted Sanpao. He strode across the hill to where his axe had fallen.

"I don't think so!" called Elenna, turning from Abraham and training her arrow on Sanpao. "One more step and I'll fire!"

The Pirate King glowered at her. "Abraham – use your axe. Kill her!"

Tom darted forwards and picked up his sword. "Elenna – be careful!" he called.

Abraham stared dizzily about himself and then dropped his axe.

"Where am I?" he mumbled.

Tom watched as the Pirate King stood seething with rage. He didn't dare to pick up his axe for fear of being shot by Elenna.

A groan from Tagus reminded Tom of how badly the Good Beast had been hurt. He ran to where the Horse-Man lay, breathing shallowly, his arms over his injured face.

Tom took the talon of Epos from his shield.

"This will help," he muttered gently, then carefully prized the Good Beast's arms from his burned face and laid the healing talon over the red-raw wounds.

Tagus let out a rasping sigh and Tom could tell that the power of the talon was already working. But he had spotted something lying in the grass where Koron had turned to dust. A fang from the Beast's mouth! Tom picked it up and tucked it into his sash, wondering what power it might have.

"Tom, the Tree!" gasped Elenna.

As he finished passing the talon over Tagus's wounds, Tom gazed back down the hill Abraham was leaning against the Tree, as though exhausted from his ordeal under Sanpao's spell. The Tree seemed to be even healthier now than when Tom had first seen it. Small green buds sprouted at the tips of the branches.

"The Tree of Being is starting to

come alive again," Tom murmured in relief. *I'll be able to open the portal and rescue Silver and my mother*. He was about to call out to Elenna to look, when the Tree shuddered from its base to its highest branches.

"No! Stay!" shouted Tom, running down the hill. But the Tree was folding in on itself, its branches closing against the trunk as it began to sink down into the ground. The whole hill shook as the Tree of Being slid swiftly into the earth with a crunching, sucking sound. A few moments later, the grass closed over it and it was as if the Tree had never even been there.

A low laugh made Tom turn angrily. Sanpao was looking gloatingly at him. "Too late!" he crowed. "I'll have that Tree for my own, yet!"

Tom glared at him. "Never," he said. "You'll be tied up and taken back to King Hugo's castle. You can share a dungeon with Malvel – the two of you should get along very well."

Sanpao lifted his head, his eyes burning with malice. "You've only faced two of my Beasts so far," he said. "There are four more – and they're far deadlier than Balisk and Koron."

"Maybe so," declared Tom. "But you'll not be free to control them!"

Sanpao laughed. "You think so?" he said, his eyes moving from Tom's face and staring at something behind and above him.

"Tom!" Elenna's voice cracked like a whip. "The pirate ship!"

Tom turned. The huge galleon was

racing across the sky, its red sails
straining as it drifted towards them.

A rope dangled from the bows.
Before Tom could act, Sanpao leaped
into the air, snatching at the rope.

With a cry of anger, Tom jumped, trying to grab at the Pirate King's boots. But he was too late – the ship was already rising again. Sanpao swarmed up the rope, as agile as a monkey. When he reached the rail, his crew helped him aboard. Then the galleon went skimming away, rising higher and higher into the sky until it was no more than a dot.

Elenna came running up to Tom. "There was nothing you could have done," she said.

A friendly roar sounded behind them. They turned and saw that Tagus was up on his hooves once more, the flesh on his face and shoulders completely healed. Tom ran over to the Good Beast. "Thank you!" he said. "We would never have succeeded without you."

Tagus bowed his head to show he understood Tom's gratitude. Then, lifting one huge hand in a gesture of farewell, he turned and galloped away across the Plains.

"What's happened?" asked a confused-looking Abraham, coming up to the two friends. "I was looking for a horse…for Blizzard. And now…"

They quickly explained how he had been under Sanpao's spell. Abraham shook his head in astonishment. "I'm glad you defeated him!" he declared. "He is an evil man!"

"He hasn't been defeated," Tom said grimly, staring up at the distant dot in the sky. "We have to follow him."

Just then, Storm and Blizzard came trotting up the hill to where they were standing – all trace of Sanpao's dark magic had disappeared from Storm's eyes.

"Take Blizzard with you," said Abraham, smiling at Elenna. "She's already taken a shine to you – you may be the one person she will allow upon her back."

"Thank you," said Elenna. She stroked the white mare's flank, then hoisted herself up into the saddle. Blizzard whickered and dipped her head as if to show Elenna that she was welcome to ride.

Saying goodbye to Abraham, Tom and Elenna cantered off side by side across the Plains in pursuit of the dwindling speck that was Sanpao's pirate ship.

"Wherever Sanpao goes, we go!" Tom said. "We'll make sure he doesn't wreak any more damage in this kingdom."

He flicked the reins, urging Storm
into a gallop. Elenna was quick to
respond and soon the two
companions were racing across the

grasslands after the ship.

While there's blood in my veins, I'll fight every Beast that Sanpao throws at me! Tom vowed.

HECTON
THE
BODY-SNATCHER

BY ADAM BLADE

ORCHARD

PROLOGUE

Sandric the Tree Dweller grabbed the vine rope that hung outside his family's hut, and swung through the Vanished Woodland. He gave a shout of exhilaration as he let go of the vine, caught hold of another, and whipped past a group of startled women sewing bark tunics. The woodland was hidden in a secret valley of Avantia, a fold in the earth tucked into the foot of the volcano. Few visitors ever came across the

Tree Dwellers. Their huts, bridges and vines, all suspended high in the canopy, had remained undisturbed for generations. Sandric had never seen anyone from outside his own tribe. He swung through the Vanished Woodland. The vine rope swept upwards in a steep arc and he let go, flinging his arms above his head. He soared like a bird above the tops of the trees, the grey slopes of the volcano looming ahead, then dropped down into the green canopy.

Branches snapped and splintered as Sandric swung among the tree tops. When he reached the glade at the centre of the Vanished Woodland, he seized a ladder woven from creepers. He scrambled up it, crawled onto a thick branch, and gasped. There it was – a tree unlike any he'd seen before.

It was enormous, its twisting branches stretched high above the canopy. The leaves were fresh and a waxy green. He gazed down the broad column of the trunk, and saw that the soil around its base was loose. The tree must have thrust, fully formed, from the ground.

But why has it come here? he wondered. A large, grey flake drifted onto the back of his hand. He sniffed it. It smelt of flame and smoke.

"The Fire Mountain is awake," he muttered.

He raised himself up on his branch and peered over the treetops. In the distance a dark cloud hung on the horizon, over the volcano. Orange flames sparked from the crater and the cloud billowed and grew, moving towards the Vanished Woodland.

More flakes of ash fluttered around him, catching on his tunic and clinging to the leaves and branches.

Sandric slid down the ladder and grabbed the vine. He swooped back among the huts, yelling, "Orange Heat! The Fire Mountain is angry!"

The other Tree Dwellers scattered, running and leaping from branch to branch to shelter inside their huts. Tendrils of smoke coiled around the trees. Sandric coughed as the acrid fumes filled his lungs. He lost his grip and slithered down the vine, almost to the ground.

A huge figure stepped out from the smoke. He had the body of a man, thickset and muscular, but with green flesh. His cloak seemed to be made from feathers and fur. It billowed out as the figure drew nearer, and

Sandric saw a fox's brush on one shoulder, a crushed rabbit on the front, and a crow dangling from the bottom. A hollowed-out bull's head formed a hood, with curled horns gleaming.

It's made from dead creatures, Sandric realised. Sweat trickled down his back.

The Beast gave a roar so loud that it seemed to shudder through Sandric. He pulled the cloak more tightly around him, and to Sandric's horror the half-rotten bodies groaned, their eyes rolling back in their heads as their gruesome stitching stretched.

Sandric was shaking so violently he could barely grip the vine. He scrambled up, his hands and feet slipping. But when he glanced to the ground, the Beast's black eyes were fixed on him, the green skin of his face contorted into a smile. In one hand he held a trident, its three points glittering through the smoke, and in the other a net fringed with metal barbs.

The Beast gave a furious hiss and

something snared around Sandric, tangling his limbs so he couldn't climb. It was the net. Sandric looked down to see the creature yank the long cord attached to the net, dragging him off the vine. He fell in a crumpled heap on the woodland floor.

"No one can help you now," the Beast mocked him, his voice deeper than the groan of a collapsing tree. "Hecton is here."

The Beast strode towards him. Sandric tried to scramble away, but with a snarl Hecton raised his trident and hurled it at him. The three blades pierced his hand, pinning Sandric to the ground. He cried out as his flesh sang with pain and blood bubbled around the three puncture wounds.

Hecton gripped the edges of his

cloak, spreading it wide, and leapt up. As the Beast flew through the air, Sandric saw more dead bodies suspended from the lining of his cloak – stoats, weasels, toads, their eyes blinking – and realised what this Beast was.

A body snatcher...

The ground shuddered as Hecton landed in a crouch over Sandric. He straddled Sandric's torso, his fists pressed into the ground either side of Sandric's head. Hecton grinned, and a trickle of yellow drool splattered onto Sandric's forehead. The Beast opened his mouth wide and a green mist wafted out, coiling around Sandric's arms and legs. The bull's head hood of his cloak fell back, revealing a writhing mass of worms instead of hair. They

wriggled free, landing on Sandric and burrowing into his flesh.

"Spare me—" Sandric started to scream. But as the mist wound down his throat, tiredness swept over him, making his eyelids droop. He stopped struggling. With a sucking noise, his body lifted into the cloak, his limbs fitting among the rotten flesh of the other creatures.

Hecton, Sandric thought. *My master.*

CHAPTER ONE

FLIGHT THROUGH THE FOG

Tom narrowed his eyes against the grey fog. Through the mist, he could see Tagus the Horse-Man cantering away across Avantia's Grassy Plains.

"Farewell!" Tom called. "And thank you."

Tagus had helped Tom and Elenna defeat Koron – an evil Beast in the thrall of Sanpao the Pirate King. Tom shuddered as he remembered Koron's deadly claws and stinging tail; Tagus had helped them defeat him.

The fog rolled in waves, weaving around Tom and Elenna's legs and making Storm and Blizzard, their two horses, whinny uneasily.

Elenna licked her finger and held it in the air. "Look," she said, showing it to Tom. It was covered in a thin coating of grit. "This isn't ordinary fog."

A distant rumble shuddered through the ground and to the east a column of orange light shot up, dazzling against the dim sky. There was an explosive roar, and a shower of grey flakes fell around them, clinging to their tunics and dusting the horses' coats. Tom coughed, wiping the dust from his eyes.

"The volcano at Stonewin is erupting," he said. "This isn't fog – it's volcanic ash."

There was another rumble, like a clap of thunder deep within the earth. Storm reared up on his hind legs, neighing with alarm.

"Easy, boy," Tom soothed his faithful stallion. To Elenna, he said, "If only I had my jewelled belt, I could ask Epos to let us know what's happening. I hope she's alright," he added. The volcano was the Flame-Bird's home.

Tom had won his magical belt many Quests ago. It was studded with jewels that afforded him special powers; the red jewel gave him the ability to understand the Beasts. But Sanpao had placed Aduro, the Good Wizard of Avantia, under an evil enchantment and Aduro had magicked the jewelled belt around Sanpao's waist, giving the Pirate King its powers. In its place, the wizard had given Tom a length of hide knotted across his waist. Tom had slotted the fang left by Koron inside it; after he defeated each of Sanpao's Beasts, it left behind a token. Each token had a mysterious power, but could only be used once.

Elenna opened Storm's saddlebag and pulled out a rolled-up map. It was made from the bark of the Tree of Being. The Tree was a magical gateway to all realms, and Sanpao and his pirate crew were determined to capture it. Possession of the Tree would allow them to loot and pillage wherever they pleased. It was Tom's Quest to stop this happening, but he and Elenna had other reasons to defeat the pirates, too; Tom's mother, Freya, and Elenna's beloved pet wolf, Silver, were trapped in the strange land of Tavania. The Tree of Being could create a portal to this other kingdom, and was their only hope of rescuing them.

Tom unfurled the map. The outline of the kingdom was etched into the bark. Tom's glance scanned the familiar landscape, where he and Elenna had shared so many adventures.

"Elenna, look at this." He jabbed a finger at the picture of a wooded valley, tucked beside the volcano. He read the lettering printed below the image. *'The Vanished Woodland.'*

"I've never heard of it before," said Elenna. "We've travelled all over

Avantia, but there are still places we haven't seen."

The tiny outline of the Tree of Being appeared at the centre of the woodland picture. The Tree didn't grow in one fixed place, but moved around so it would be safe from attack. It sprang from the ground, fully formed, before disappearing into the earth once more. Tom and Elenna had to travel quickly to each new

location to reach it before the pirates.

"So that's where we need to go," said Tom.

"And where we'll meet the next Beast," Elenna added.

Tom nodded. After they defeated Koron, Sanpao had warned that the next Beast they faced would be the most terrible yet.

Tom returned the map to Storm's saddlebag.

The stallion tossed his head, flicking away ash. Tom patted his flank before hoisting himself on to his back. Elenna climbed on to Blizzard. The snow-white mare had been given to her by Abraham the Horse-Whisperer, who they'd rescued from Sanpau's thrall. Blizzard shied away from the tumbling ash, whinnying fearfully. Elenna leaned low over her, stroking her mane as she murmured reassuring words.

"She's getting used to you," Tom grinned as Blizzard calmed down. "Silver will be jealous."

Elenna looked down at the ground. Tom felt a tug of guilt.

"You'll see him again," he promised. "We'll defeat Sanpao and get Silver and my mother back."

They cantered northwest across the Grassy Plains. The nearer they got to the volcano, the thicker the ash hung in the air. It was becoming warmer, too; Tom could feel the dust sticking to his damp skin. Elenna's face was streaked with grime, like she'd fallen into a pile of cinders. A puff of flakes swirled around them, and Tom spluttered as they filled his lungs.

"Pull your collar up," called Elenna,

yanking her own over her nose and
mouth. Tom did the same, and found
he could breathe more easily. They
reached into Storm's saddlebags,
taking out the blankets they slept in
at night. They draped them over the
noses of their horses and secured
them in the bridles.

They galloped through the rippling
expanse of grass, soaring over ditches
and wading through streams. They
had been travelling for almost a full
day when the ground became firmer,
and the horses' hooves clattered over
rocks and pebbles. Looming through
the ash was a distant village.

"I know this place," Tom called
across to Elenna. "We're north of the
Forest of Fear."

He raised a hand above his eyes,
squinting. He could make out

half-collapsed buildings. Plumes of smoke billowed from them, mingling with the ash in the sky.

"What happened?" Elenna wondered.

They drew closer and saw a column of people pouring out of the village. Men and women were carrying bundles on their backs. They could hear the sobs and cries of children as their parents hurried them along. A shout rose up from among the villagers:

"Look – they've come to help us! Over here! Please help."

The people rushed towards them through the ash and thronged about Storm and Blizzard, their faces pale and their eyes wide with terror.

A bearded man stepped up to Tom. "Our village has been ransacked by a— Oh, it was terrible!" The man broke down, sobbing.

Tom felt sure he knew who had harmed these people. There was only one group of men capable of such evil in Avantia.

"Pirates," Tom muttered. "Elenna, this is all down to Sanpao's men!"

CHAPTER TWO

THE RAIDED VILLAGE

"We were sheltering indoors from the ash cloud," said a woman with a baby on her hip. "They helped themselves to our food – and then they tore apart our houses." The mother glanced at the child she was holding, her face crumpling. "They snatched my boy," she said. "I couldn't hold on to him! Not with this one to carry."

"A recruit, they said!" hissed the bearded man. "A pirate recruit!"

Tom looked at Elenna. They both knew what it was to be torn from their families. *I won't let this happen to the children of Avantia*, Tom thought.

Tom drew his sword. "Head for the western shore," he told the villagers. "That should be far enough away from the pirates. While there's blood in my veins, we won't rest until we've defeated them."

As the villagers did as Tom asked, the woman with the baby looked up at Tom. Tears were running down her face. "Those pirates have my Aaron," she said. "Please find him!"

Tom thought of his mother and Silver, so far from home. "We'll get him back," he said. "I swear it."

Storm and Blizzard cantered to the ruined village. Tom glanced back and saw the woman watching them go, her baby clasped to her. He drew his collar up, squinting against the swirling flakes of ash. The sun was starting to set, tingeing the grey sky with orange. As they approached the village, he saw that most of it had been reduced to piles of rubble.

A flag had been hoisted up one of the remaining towers, emblazoned with the outline of a Beast's skull. *Sanpao's symbol*, Tom thought.

Elenna was pointing at the defensive wall that circled the village. "Look," she said.

It was lined with Sanpao's pirates. Weapons gleamed cruelly in their hands – Tom could see crossbows and cat-o'-nine-tails, even heavy iron balls swung on chains. The same skull symbol was tattooed on their chests in ebony ink.

"Hold it straight, brat," one of the pirates bawled. Tom saw a young boy standing among them, struggling to hold a cutlass. It was almost as large as he was. "Want your mummy to help?" the pirate sneered. "Well, guess what? She's not here!" The pirates cackled with laughter.

"That must be Aaron," Elenna said. Her eyes flashed angrily. "Where's Sanpao?"

"I can't see him anywhere," Tom replied, scanning the row of men for the Pirate King. "Maybe he's left them here to loot while he goes after the Tree."

Tom had to get the new recruit away – and then track down Sanpao

and the Tree of Life. He and Elenna
halted in front of the village gate. The
pirates leered down at them, laughing
and brandishing their weapons.

"Look who it is! Not learnt your
lesson yet, you scrawny scallywags?"
the pirate who had been mocking
Aaron yelled. His gold tooth glittered
in the light from the setting sun.

Another man, with a long scar

around his neck, flicked his cat-o'-nine-tails towards Tom and Elenna. "I reckon they be wanting a taste of my cat."

As the pirates laughed darkly, Tom raised his sword. "Cowards! You can't loot defenceless villagers and steal their children!"

"Oh, can't we?" said the pirate with the gold tooth. He held his arms wide, gesturing to the other men. "You may not have noticed, you poxy dogs, but we're pirates! Stealing and looting is what we do." He grabbed Aaron's shoulder. "This brat here's just the start," he said. "We'll soon have a new crew of boys trained up."

The pirate with the scar slapped him on the back. As they laughed and hooted, Tom saw a dark shape snaking down from the wall towards

Elenna. A lasso! It looped over her body and pulled tight, forcing her arms to her side.

"Looks like we've got ourselves another recruit, lads," laughed the scared pirate, yanking on the lasso and dragging Elenna towards the wall. She writhed and kicked.

"Get this off me!" she yelled.

With a cry, Tom flung his sword towards the lasso. It spun through the air, blade flashing, and sliced the cords of rope.

"You won't get away next time," snarled the pirate.

Tom picked up his sword and cut through the loop around Elenna.

"Thanks," Elenna said. "How are we going to get past them to rescue Aaron? They've got numbers and a vantage point on their side."

An idea started to form in Tom's mind. "The pirates are trying to capture people, but perhaps we need to play them at their own game. Every village has a prison, doesn't it?" he asked.

Elenna nodded.

"Remember when we first met Tagus, and we were locked up? Maybe we can find a way to get the pirates locked up, too. Then we can save Aaron – and get some of Sanpao's men out of the way. It'll make the rest of our Quest easier."

Elenna's eyes gleamed. "I like it! Prison's the least they deserve."

"We'll come back at night," Tom said. They mounted Storm and Blizzard and rode away from the village wall. Dusk was falling, the sky a leaden grey.

"Gone so soon, you lily-livered cowards?" one of the pirates yelled after them. A bottle whistled past them, shattering on the ground.

Not for long, Tom thought. *Just you wait.*

CHAPTER THREE

LOOTING THE PIRATES

Tom and Elenna set up camp behind a cluster of boulders, out of view of the village. The ash-sprinkled ground was covered in footprints, which Tom guessed had been made by the fleeing villagers.

Elenna and Tom settled down to a simple supper by the camp fire Tom had lit. Its flames were dwarfed by the fountains of lava shooting up from the volcano, casting a garish light across the sky. *The Tree of Being is out there somewhere*, Tom thought uneasily. *I just hope Sanpao hasn't found it yet.*

"So how are we going to get the pirates into prison?" Elenna asked between mouthfuls.

Tom took a gulp of water from his flask. "With the amount of food and drink they've stolen, they'll be guzzling away. They'll soon be fast asleep. Let's take their weapons and use them to lure the pirates into prison," Tom replied.

Elenna's eyes were bright with amusement. "We'll be looting the looters!"

Tom jumped to his feet. "It's dark enough now," he said. "Come on – the sooner we do this, the sooner we can get on with our Quest. And Sanpao will have fewer men to stop us."

Elenna kicked dirt over the fire to extinguish it. Tom swung his shield over his shoulder, put one foot into Storm's stirrup, and grabbed the reins to pull himself up.

They cantered towards the village walls. Tom squinted in the darkness. The walls were empty of pirates now. Tom and Elenna halted the horses and listened for a few moments. It was silent, save for the dull rumble of the volcano.

"The pirates must be sleeping off everything they've eaten," whispered Tom.

He guided Storm so the stallion was standing right against the wall. Tom stood up in the saddle and reached for the wall's top, gripping a ridge in the stonework. He bent his knees then sprang up, hooking his left leg over the wall. He scrambled across it and leaped down, landing on a platform. A flight of stone steps led down into the streets. Torches hung among the scorched and damaged buildings. Their faint glow was enough for Tom to make out heaps of rubble and an open space in the centre, which he guessed was the village square.

He looked back over the wall to see Elenna already standing on Storm's saddle. He leaned down towards her, his hand outstretched. She grabbed it, and used her feet to scale the wall while Tom pulled her over.

They crept down the steps and into the village streets. Elenna tugged at

Tom's sleeve and pointed at a thick wall and wooden door set underneath the flight of stairs. There were bars in the tiny window at the top of the door.

"The prison," she whispered.

The door was ajar, the key dangling in the lock. On either side of the frame was a wooden slot, into which a plank could be fitted to make the door secure. Tom pushed it open and peered inside, wincing as the hinges creaked. He grinned. "Perfect – it's empty."

They turned back to face the village square and carefully stepped through torn-down houses and lanes littered with upturned barrels of food.

Tom could hear a rasping noise coming from the direction of the village square.

"Sounds like snoring," he murmured.
He and Elenna made their way
towards the square. They ducked
behind a broken cart and peered out.
The market stalls had hammocks
strung between them, and in each
slept a snoring pirate. Some mumbled
in their sleep, while others scratched

and twitched. One gave a belch and rubbed his belly. "Cursed Avantian grub," he muttered in his sleep.

Tom silently beckoned Elenna forward. They crept out from behind the cart and among the pirates. In a far corner of the square, Tom saw a small figure huddled on the ground – Aaron. His cheeks shone damply in the torchlight, and Tom guessed that he'd cried himself to sleep.

Some of Sanpao's crew had their weapons with them in their hammocks, but most had strewn them on the ground. Tom could see that Elenna already had a crossbow and a cutlass. He ducked to pick up a dagger from underneath a hammock, careful not to disturb the pirate sleeping above it, drool trickling from his open mouth.

Tom shoved the dagger into his hide belt and picked up a cat-o'-nine-tails leaning against a post. The pirate in the next hammock let out great, grunting snores. His mouth gaped and Tom caught the glint of a gold tooth in the moonlight.

Our friend from earlier, he thought. *And what have we here?*

Nestled by one of the pirate's thick arms was a cutlass with a golden blade.

Slowly, Tom took hold of it, gently teasing the weapon out of the hammock. He grinned when it came clear, turning the cutlass in his hand. Its gleaming blade was engraved with intricate patterns, its hilt studded with jewels.

Who did you steal this from? Tom wondered.

But as he stepped away, his foot nudged one of the bottles on the ground. It rolled into the metal frame of the market stall with a clank.

The gold-toothed pirate jerked bolt upright. "What scurvy dog goes there?" he snarled.

CHAPTER FOUR

THE TRAP
IS SET

Tom dropped to the ground and
rolled under the hammock. He lay
still, his heart hammering as the
pirate shifted around. Across the
square he could see that Elenna had
crouched low at the foot of one of
the posts. There was a swishing
sound as the pirate drew his dagger;
above him, Tom could see his

outstretched arm, jabbing the air with his blade.

"Cursed land's got me imagining things," muttered the pirate. The hammock swung as he lay back down again. "Sooner we find that Tree the better." With a snort, the rise and fall of his snores soon started again.

Tom exhaled a long sigh of relief. He saw Elenna get to her feet and he rolled out, the cutlass still in his hand. He moved quickly around the other hammocks, gathering the remaining weapons, then knelt beside Aaron. He shook the boy's shoulder gently.

Aaron's eyes flew open. Tom clamped a hand over his mouth before he could cry out.

"It's OK," Tom whispered. "We're here to rescue you. Follow me."

Aaron nodded, and they hurried through the square, ducking behind the broken cart. Elenna squatted down beside them, her arms full of blades and arrows. One of Tom's cutlasses clanked against a crossbow, the sound like a bell ringing across the dark square. They stiffened, but the pirates carried on snoring.

"That was close," Elenna whispered.

"We're going to get the pirates out of the way now," Tom explained to Aaron. "Stay out of sight – and use this if you have to." He gave him a dagger, then turned to Elenna. "Come on, let's get our loot to the prison."

They crept out of the square and back through the ruined streets. Once they reached the cell under the stone steps, Tom opened the creaking door and they piled the weapons at the back. The torches outside made them gleam.

"It looks just like a pile of treasure," Tom said. "The pirates are sure to take a look. I'll go and wake them up, then run on ahead and hide there." He pointed to the space behind the door. "You can wait on the steps above us with this." Tom passed Elenna one of the looted blades, a long rapier that would fit across the slots on either side of the door. "Once the pirates are inside, I'll run out, and you jump down to help me lock the door."

Elenna tilted her head. "Sounds good – except for one thing." She pressed the rapier back into Tom's hand. "I should be the one who wakes the pirates and hides in here."

"But that means you'll be in the most danger, and—"

"Look at the space behind the door," Elenna interrupted. "It's tiny. I'm smaller than you, so I should be the one who hides there."

Tom grinned and nodded. Not for the first time, he felt lucky to have Elenna with him on his Quests.

He watched her set off back to the square, and when she was out of sight he climbed up the steps. Fresh flakes of ash had already covered the footprints he and Elenna had left earlier. Tom leaned over the edge of the steps, checking he was directly above the cell door. Then he crouched down, the rapier by his side.

"Ahoy there, you lily-livered lot!" The voice split through the night air. Then Elenna came back into view, sprinting towards the cell. To Tom's amazement, she paused and yelled in a voice lower than her usual tone, "There be a crock of booty awaiting us!"

Tom had to stifle a laugh. His friend was pretending to be a pirate!

The pirates staggered up the street after Elenna, yawning and stretching. But their pace quickened when

Elenna shouted, "It's in this here cell," and darted inside.

"Look at that, lads!" shouted the pirate with the scar on his face. "Gold! We're going to be the richest crew that ever sailed the skies."

The torchlight lit up their grins and shining eyes as they shoved and jostled their way in after Elenna. Tom hoped she'd had time to hide properly. He drew himself up, ready to spring.

"That's not booty," Tom heard another of the pirates yell. "They're our weapons!"

Elenna shot out of the prison. Tom sprang from the steps on to the ground beside her, the rapier in his hand. They both slammed the door shut.

"What's going on?" one of the

trapped pirates yelled.

"Quick," gasped Tom, as the pirates
started shoving against the door.

He and Elenna slid the rapier into
the wooden slots on each side of the
door frame, holding it fast. Tom
turned the key in the lock and tucked

it into his jerkin. The pirates kicked and punched from the other side, but the door didn't budge.

One of the pirates looked out of the window by the window.

"You wait until we get out of here," he pirate hissed. "We'll dip you in a pot of boiling tar and toss you off our ship. You'll be sorry you were born!"

"You'll be the sorry ones, matey," retorted Elenna in her pirate voice.

The two of them ran back to the square. "Sanpao's a few men down now," Tom gasped as they dashed along the street. "And they won't be snatching any more children for their crew."

"Aaron!" Elenna called as they reached the square. "You're safe!"

The boy peered out from behind the cart. Then he broke into a grin of delight and rushed towards them.

"You do a good pirate's voice!" he told Elenna with a wide smile. Elenna gave him a hug and tousled his hair. "Let's get you out of here."

They raced up the stone steps to the wall and scrambled over it. Tom whistled to Storm and Blizzard and they trotted over.

"What were you doing all the way over there?" wondered Elenna, smoothing Blizzard's mane.

"Hiding," said Tom grimly, crouching to look at footprints in the ash. The soles each had the outline of the Beast's skull. "More pirates must have passed this way. Lots of them." Tom stood and followed the trail with his eyes. His chest tightened. "They're heading towards the Vanished Woodland – and the Tree of Being. There's no time to waste."

Elenna glanced towards Aaron, who was stroking Storm's muzzle. "We can't bring him with us," she said quietly. "It's too dangerous."

A figure stepped out from behind a mound of rocks. Tom's hand curled around his sword, but a flash of fire from the volcano lit the sky. It was Aaron's mother, her baby clutched to her hip. With a cry, she ran towards Aaron and embraced him.

"Thank you!" she said to Tom and Elenna. "How can I ever repay you?"

"By safely reaching the western shore," Tom said.

He and Elenna watched the woman and her children disappear.

"That's one person freed from the pirates," Tom said. "Now we need to save the rest of the kingdom."

CHAPTER FIVE

THE VANISHED WOODLAND

"Tom...Tom!" Elenna was calling to him.

He opened his eyes. The early morning light was made as dingy as ditchwater by the ash suspended in the sky. They'd travelled through most of the night and were now much closer to the volcano. Fountains of burning lava still erupted from its crater.

"We must be near the Vanished Woodland," said Elenna. She pointed at the footprints that snaked across the ground ahead, bearing the tell-tale skull pattern. "These tracks come from another direction. Sanpao must have looting parties all over Avantia."

Tom noticed a grey-green shadow at the foot of the mountain. It was a band of trees, their branches quivering. The light shifted, and the shadow faded, but then reappeared – as soft as a ribbon of silk. It was a forest, taking form and then vanishing again.

"There it is!" Tom cried. "The Vanished Woodland."

"I can guess how it got its name," said Elenna with a grin.

It wasn't until they reached the outskirts of the woodland that it seemed to stay solid. The ash was denser the closer they came to the volcano, and Tom saw that both the pirates' prints and those left by the horses were as deep as the length of his thumb. Elenna's eyes were red and watery and Tom's mouth and nose felt full of the bitter-tasting flakes. Every leaf and branch of the woodland was veiled with ash. It lay heaped on the ground like snow. Flowers bent under its weight.

Somewhere in there was the Tree of Being, Tom thought. *But where?*

They left Storm and Blizzard on the edge of the forest, somewhere sheltered from the ash so they could breathe. "Stay here and rest, boy," said Tom, patting Storm's long, black neck. He whinnied and nuzzled Tom's hair while Elenna patted

Blizzard farewell.

Tom and Elenna stepped among the trees. The wisps of ash trailing from their leaves and falling in grey showers made the trees look like rows of spectres. The pirates' footprints led deep into the woodland. Tom and Elenna followed, checking around them for signs of movement.

"If the pirates are here, the next Beast won't be far away," said Tom. He drew his sword, while Elenna fitted an arrow to her bow.

They were coming towards a glade. Tom gasped. In the centre of a clearing, through the rows of whitened trunks, he could see one that was brown. It towered high above the other trees, its trunk as broad as Tom's arm-span. The bark

gleamed like polished leather.
Clusters of dark green buds uncurled
into leaves, sparkling like ornate
shards of emerald.

"The Tree of Being," Tom breathed.
They went up to its trunk, running

their hands over the smooth, dark surface.

"I can hardly believe it was a withered, spindly thing when we first saw it," said Elenna.

"It's becoming stronger with each Quest we complete," Tom replied. "If we manage to drive Sanpao from the kingdom, maybe its full strength will return."

And I will have my mother back, he thought. He pictured her strong, noble face. Did she know that Tom was thinking of her – and trying to save her?

But while they had been standing by the Tree, dense swirls of ash had closed around them. Tom could only just make out the other trees in the woodland. His skin prickled all over. An instinct honed over many Quests told him that something evil lurked nearby, hidden in the ash.

Whoosh! A net flashed down by his left shoulder. It snared onto the tokens on his shield and whipped back up, dragging it into the branches.

CHAPTER SIX

HECTON ATTACKS

Tom held out his sword, whirling round as he stared up into the thick ash. It was making his eyes stream, but even when he wiped them with his sleeve he still couldn't see where his shield had gone. Elenna trained an arrow upwards, but she aimed it uncertainly from side to side.

Tom sheathed his blade and peered

upwards. The clouds seemed less heavy around the woodland canopy. Tom seized hold of the trunk of a tree, making its ash coat shower away. It was sturdy, but narrow enough for him to grip its sides with his arms and legs.

"I'm going up," he said. "No one steals my shield!"

He shimmied up the trunk. Elenna scaled the tree beside him, nimbly seizing a low branch and hoisting herself on to it. As Tom climbed, the ash thinned, and he could see through the Vanished Woodland.

"Tom!" Elenna called in surprise.

He followed the line of her pointed finger and saw a hut built around the top of a tree trunk. Its walls were woven from thin branches, and the leaf-covering of the roof was just visible underneath its dusting of ash. Its door gaped open, showing a drift of dust gathered inside. In the distance he could make out more huts, clustered throughout the canopy, their doors open, too.

"These huts look like they've been

recently abandoned," Tom said.

"Maybe they left to escape the ash," suggested Elenna. "Or..."

They stared at each other.

"Or to escape Sanpao's Beast," Tom finished.

They climbed higher. As he heaved himself through the branches, Tom peered across the canopy. "It's no good," he called to Elenna. "I still can't see anything."

But Elenna was staring at the ground beneath them, her face pale.

Tom looked down. A ripple of green mist was curling through the ash cloud. It looked like a blemish of mould, twisting and coiling towards them. As it drifted around Tom's feet he suddenly clamped his hand over his mouth and nose. His stomach writhed. The green mist gave off a stench like rotting flesh.

The mist seemed to slice the ash cloud away, then vanished to reveal a tall figure. At first Tom thought it was a huntsman. But as the plumes of ash cleared, he saw that the figure's flesh was a putrid green, and hanging from its belt was the net – and Tom's shield. The creature's mouth gaped open, and the green mist was billowing out. His dark eyes stared directly up at Tom.

He glanced at Elenna, who held her sleeve over her mouth and nose. She nodded, and he knew she was thinking the same as him: *Sanpao's Beast.*

A breeze shivered through the woodland, flapping the Beast's cape. It was sewn from the bodies of dozens of creatures. Tom could see

tails and ears and feathers, all
meshed together in a tapestry of
death. At the top of the cape,
hollowed out to form a hood, was a
horned bull's head. Flies buzzed over
the cape's decaying surface and blood
and pus dripped down it.

With a snarl that made the
branches shudder, the Beast leapt
into the air, his cape flying out
behind him. He landed on the trunk
of Tom's tree, slamming into it with
a force that made the branches shake
and quiver. His mouth twisted into
a grin and he climbed up towards
Tom, gripping the bark with his
clawed hands, his movements as
smooth as a spider's.

"Hecton comes for you," the
Beast growled. "I will snatch
your body and you will join the

other wretched creatures."

Tom tried to climb away from Hecton, but the spindly topmost branches snapped. He could see Elenna scrambling out along a branch, trying to reach him. It dipped under her weight, forcing her back towards the trunk.

"There's no escape," mocked Hecton. Puffs of mist escaped his mouth when he spoke.

Tom heard pitiful groans and cries, and realised they were coming from the creatures in the cape. Their glassy eyes rolled and he saw that the stitching which passed through their bodies was stretched taut.

The Beast had almost reached him. The horns on the bull's head would soon be close enough to stab his feet. Tom looked around wildly. Elenna's face in the next tree was white with horror. He couldn't go up, and the other trees were too far away to jump to.

He was trapped.

This may be the last Beast I face, Tom thought, *but I'll fight to the end.*

CHAPTER SEVEN

A VOICE ON THE AIR

Gripping the tree with one hand, he drew his sword with the other, pointing it down towards Hecton. "Stay back!" he shouted.

The Beast laughed, a gurgling sound like a creature being sucked into a marsh. He reached into his cape and brought out a trident, its three prongs glittering. With a growl

he pulled his fist back over his
shoulder.

"Tom, look out!" yelled Elenna
from her tree.

Hecton flung the trident at him.
Tom twisted aside and it thudded into
the spot where he'd been. Its points
were embedded into the bark,
snaring the edge of his jerkin. Tom
seized the hilt of the trident, trying to
prise it free, but it wouldn't budge.
Not only was he trapped at the top of
the tree – now he was pinned against
the trunk.

Panic fluttered inside him as
Hecton clambered
even closer. The
stench of the
Beast's

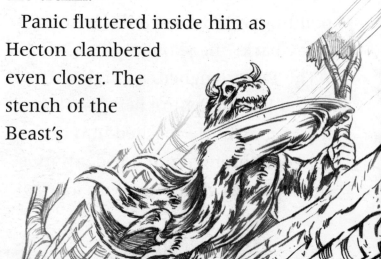

rotting cloak was making him feel sick. He turned his sword upside-down, so he could slice through his jerkin with its blade, but his head

was swimming, and he fumbled his grip.

His sword spun through the ash cloud to the ground.

Trapped. And unarmed...

Tom had never felt more helpless. Hecton was grinning up at him. The eyes of the mangled creatures sewn into his cape rolled back into their skulls. He could feel sweat trickling down his face as a surge of nausea rose in his throat. He closed his eyes, shivering.

"No, Tom!" Elenna shouted.

He gulped down the sickness, forcing his eyes open to see an arrow whizz towards the tree. It flew past Hecton's face, scratching the green skin.

Elenna! She was crouched on a sturdy branch, her bow raised.

Hecton's clawed hand reached up towards him and Tom kicked it away. The Beast slipped a little down the tree and Elenna loosed another arrow. Hecton snarled as he swiped it aside.

"Catch, Tom!" Elenna shouted.

She shot another arrow. Tom followed its flight, his eyes narrowed intently. *If I miss, it's all over*, he thought.

As the arrow hurtled towards him, Tom lunged out as far as the trident would let him and snatched at it. The plummeting shaft slid through his fingers with burning speed, but he closed his fist around the feathers at the arrow's base.

"Good work!" he called to Elenna.

He held onto one of the branches, gritting his teeth as he used the point of the arrow to slice through his jerkin. The fabric gave way and he jerked downwards, tossing the arrow to the ground so he could hold on to the tree with both hands.

"Look out, Tom!" Elenna yelled. "The mist!"

Hecton let out a roar of anger, his green features contorted. Mist wafted from his jaws with a hissing sound. It curled around his ankles like the tendrils of a creeping plant. Through the green haze, he saw Hecton lower his hood. His scalp writhed with the squelching bodies of hundreds of worms. They surged down the Beast's arms, dragging themselves on to the trunk and wriggling up towards Tom. They were greyish-white, their circular jaws edged with tiny, jagged teeth.

Like maggots, Tom thought. Hecton breathed another gust of green mist, which flowed around Tom's chest and face. His eyes slid shut as it filled his lungs. He was suddenly so tired. Elenna's voice rang out, high and panicked, but he didn't reply. Hecton wouldn't want him to. *And I want to please Hecton*... he thought sleepily.

"Tom!" It was a man's voice, distant and faint. "Tom, you

must fight the Beast's evil."

Tom's eyes flew open. He would know that voice anywhere. "Aduro!"

"I am by your side once more," came the Good Wizard's voice. "I am fighting Sanpao's spell – and now you must fight his body-snatcher..."

"Aduro, where are you?" Tom cried, twisting about in the tree as he searched for some sign of the Good Wizard.

A stab of pain dragged him back to the battle. The first of the worms had reached him. Its jaws fixed on the back of his hand, biting and sucking the skin. He punched it away with his other hand and kicked at the worms crawling about his feet. Hecton growled angrily and the creatures in his cape moaned, their eyes gummy from the green mist.

Body-snatcher! Suddenly Tom understood. Those animals had already had their bodies snatched. If he didn't get away from the green mist and writhing worms, his own rotting carcass would be stitched into the cape, too – where he would remain forever.

CHAPTER EIGHT

SANPAO'S THREAT

I can't go up, and I can't jump sideways, Tom thought. He looked down at the ground. *There's one way out of this...*

He let go of the trunk.

As he hurtled towards Hecton, Tom stretched out and gripped the top of his shield, yanking it from the Beast's belt. The force of his fall tore Hecton from the tree. Tom heard the Beast's snarl of anger as they tumbled over and over together. Hecton's rotten cape flapped over Tom's face, making him gag, and the Beast gripped his arm. With a shout, Tom drew up his legs and thumped them into Hecton's neck. The Beast gave a howl of pain, releasing Tom's arm, and spinning into a cloud of ash.

Tom knew he only had moments before he would slam into the

ground. He twisted in mid-air, fixing the shield to his arm, and called on the power of Arcta's eagle feather. He plunged through the ash cloud and landed on his side in a mulch of damp leaves. He rolled over and got to his feet, unhurt; the feather had done its job.

"Tom!" he heard Elenna call. She appeared through the ash cloud, sliding down the trunk of her tree to the ground. "Where's Hecton?"

Tom whirled around, but there was no sign of the Beast.

Boooom... An explosive rumble sounded in the distance, casting a flash of blue light through the ash.

"That wasn't the volcano," Elenna said, gripping her bow.

Tom shook his head grimly. "It's coming from the village."

Elenna's eyes widened. "The pirates...?"

"That's right, little girl!" crowed a voice from high up in the woodland's canopy. "I heard about your stunt in the village, and my crew are blasting their way free. Gunpowder isn't just for cannons."

Tom grabbed his sword from where it had fallen at the foot of the Tree. He and Elenna peered into the trees, Elenna pointing an arrow upwards.

"Come on, Sanpao!" Tom yelled. "Show yourself!"

The Pirate King let out a booming laugh. "What, and spoil Hecton's fun? How do you like his cape, by the way? He wants a new tunic now. Just picture it – he could make sleeves out of your arms and legs, and use your heads for pockets."

A curl of green mist reached down towards them like a rotting finger. It wrapped around Elenna's neck and head, and to Tom's horror his friend's eyes drooped.

"Sleepy," she mumbled and staggered to one side.

Tom grabbed her shoulders and shook her. "Elenna, no!" He remembered Aduro's words. "You have to fight it."

There were flecks of white in the mist, and Tom realised that the deadly worms were dropping down around them. One had clambered onto Elenna's leg. It arched its spine and sank its jaws into the muscle behind her calf. It twisted, burrowing inside her skin. She gave a gasp of pain.

Tom lunged down and prised it away with the flat of his blade. He swept his shield through the green mist, scattering it into hundreds of tiny puffs. Somewhere in the mist around them, he heard Hecton snarl.

Elenna's eyes fluttered open. "Thanks," she said groggily. "Now let's finish this."

"My pleasure!" Sanpao yelled.

The ash-smothered woodland came to life. Pirates whipped through the trees towards Tom and Elenna, swinging on long vines. They whooped and cheered, singing snatches of song: *"Scourge of land, of sky and sea, the Pirates of Makai are we!"*

The men released their hold on the vines and dropped to the ground, kicking up clouds of ash. Another figure swung down towards them, larger than the others, and roared a battle cry that echoed through the

Vanished Woodland – Sanpao. He flipped through the air, turning over and landing in a crouch beside the Tree of Being. He had an enormous axe in his hand, its blade edged with what looked like shark's teeth.

"Ahoy, my young friends," Sanpao sneered to Tom and Elenna. He drew himself up to his full height. "I'm glad you're here to see my victory."

His tattooed arms and plaited coil of hair shone greasily, and the jewels in Tom's belt glittered. The Pirate King raised his axe above his head. His shoulder muscles rippled as he swung it at the Tree of Being.

"No!" yelled Tom. He hurled his sword at Sanpao. The hilt clattered against his fist, making the axe fall from his grasp. It missed the Tree, slicing harmlessly into the ground.

Sanpao's oily plait swung like a whip as he twisted round to face Tom. "You dirty dog," he snarled. He pulled out a dagger. "By the time I've finished, Hecton won't be able to make a handkerchief from what's left of your sorry, snivelling body." He charged at Tom, the dagger aimed at his chest. Tom leapt up and grasped the lowest branch of the Tree of Being. He swung his legs, wrapping them around the branch, and pulled himself on to it. He held his arms outstretched, balancing on the smooth, brown surface. Sanpao skidded to a halt and turned back, his face crumpled with rage.

"And by the time we're finished, Sanpao," Tom said, "you'll wish you'd never heard of Avantia!"

CHAPTER NINE

BATTLE AMONG THE TREES

Tom could sense the air throbbing around him and the branch beneath his feet vibrated and hummed. Something was happening.

The Tree's giving me strength, he realised. *It wants me to defeat Sanpao.*

The Pirate King was snarling up at him. His crew circled around the Tree, and one of them charged at Elenna with his cutlass. Stepping nimbly aside, she slashed an arrow at him like a dagger; the tip grazed his thick neck, making him drop his weapon. His cry of surprise made Sanpao glance towards him.

Tom leapt from the branch, landing on Sanpao's shoulders. The Pirate King crumpled, striking his head on an exposed tree root. Tom jumped clear as his enemy leaped to his feet. Sanpao's eyes were dark with hatred. He rushed at Tom, his dagger thrust out towards him. Tom jumped and caught hold of the branch again, drawing up his knees and thumping his feet into Sanpao's chest. The Pirate King staggered backwards, his breath coming in harsh rasps.

Elenna shot at a pirate attempting to fix an arrow to a crossbow,

splintering its wooden frame. Other
pirates emerged through the
Vanished Woodland, and Tom
guessed they were the men he and
Elenna had imprisoned.

One of them shoved the pirate with
the crossbow aside. "I'll be dealing
with this scurvy scum," he said, and
Tom recognised the glitter of his gold
tooth when he spoke.

In the pirate's hand was a spiked ball and chain. He advanced on Elenna, whirling it above his head as another of Sanpao's crew charged her from the side, aiming a cat-o'-nine-tails. She needed help – and quickly...

Tom reached for his sword, but it wasn't hanging by his hip. *Oh no*, he thought, remembering that it was still lying where he had thrown it at Sanpao's axe. But there was something tucked into his hide belt. *Of course – Koron's fang!*

He pulled out the fang and hurled it at the gold-toothed pirate. It spun over and over on itself as it sliced through the air, then struck the pirate on the side of his neck. He dropped his ball and chain. The fang disappeared, leaving a black mark, like mildew, on the pirate's skin. His body was rigid, his mouth frozen mid-shout, his eyes unblinking, limbs unmoving. He toppled to the ground and lay as stiffly as a fallen tree.

"I can't move!" he shouted. "Help!"

"Thanks, Tom," called Elenna, as the pirate grunted and growled. "Looks like we won't have to worry about him for a while."

She swivelled, training her bow on the pirate with the cat-o'-nine-tails. But he was staring at his frozen companion. With a cry of terror, he hurtled off through the trees.

"Where do you think you're off to?" Sanpao bellowed after him. "Yellow-dog coward!"

Tom ran and picked up his sword. The Pirate King had yanked his shark's tooth axe from the ground and slung it over his shoulder. They stood on either side of the Tree of Being, slowly circling the trunk.

"You don't give up, do you?" Sanpao said, his cruel mouth curled into a sneer.

Tom shook his head. "Never. I would fight to the death to rid Avantia of you."

Sanpao laughed – a long bellow of mirth that seemed to rattle in his chest like a box of bones.

"Surely you can't really believe that your silly Quests are worth dying for?" asked Sanpao.

Tom nodded. "I'm fighting for my kingdom – and my mother. I would gladly give my life for either."

"Well, I'll help you prove it some time," said Sanpao. "But not now."

The Pirate King clicked his fingers. The swirling clouds of ash lifted, cleaved apart by the pirates' floating ship. Its wooden hull creaked as it lowered down towards them. Its masts were hung with red and black sails, each marked with the Beast skull symbol. The largest mast was a branch Sanpao had already stolen from the Tree of Being. Cannons were visible through the hatches in the ship's sides, and it was encrusted all over with metal spikes.

The pirates already on board tossed ropes over the side, which snaked down to the ground. The crew seized hold of them, clambering up hand over hand and on to the ship. Sanpao gave Tom and Elenna a mocking salute, grabbed one of the ropes, and hoisted himself up.

Tom watched him, leaning on his sword. "Wait!" he called as something occurred to him. "Did you make the volcano erupt?"

Sanpao paused and looked down, grinning. "Of course I did! Who else would want to empty the region and steal its loot? I told you my gunpowder was useful. I dropped a load of it inside the crater and – boom! I made my very own volcanic eruption. Ask your wizard about it – if you ever see him again."

With a final laugh, he scrambled up the rope, after the other pirates, and on to the ship. It rose up, until it seemed the size of a bird, and drifted out of sight.

Elenna was holding a bundle of arrows, wiping their tips clean with her sleeve. She walked towards Tom, a puzzled frown on her face. "Why didn't you try to stop Sanpao?" she asked.

Tom turned to gaze over the woodland. "We've still got a Beast to face," he said.

CHAPTER TEN

THE CREATURES IN THE CAPE

"If we don't defeat Hecton, he'll kill every creature he can," Tom said. "We've seen how dangerous he is."

Elenna nodded. "You're right."

Tom saw the Beast moving towards them through the trees, just visible through a shroud of green mist.

"Duck!" he yelled.

Elenna flung herself to the ground and Tom hurled his shield, sending it spinning towards the Beast. Hecton gave a howl of pain as the shield struck his midriff, and he sank to his knees. As Tom and Elenna charged towards him, Tom saw that the Beast had a jagged branch stuck through his upper arm. *That must have happened when he fell*, Tom realised.

The green mist coiled around Hecton, and the white worms from his head tumbled onto his body, nibbling at his skin with their circular jaws. Hecton groaned and batted them away. He sank to his knees, the mist making his eyes roll shut.

"That's it!" Tom called to Elenna. "Our weapons can only do so much. We have to get Hecton to turn his magic on himself – make the Beast devour his own body!"

When they reached the struggling

Beast, Tom darted around him, dodging his flailing limbs. As Hecton reached upwards, Tom snatched the net from where it was hooked inside his belt. Elenna ran behind Hecton. The worms were crawling over his injured arm, and when the Beast curled up with a bellow of pain, Tom threw the net over him. Elenna caught it and pulled an arrow from her quiver, using it to pin the net to the ground. Tom stretched his side of the net taut and rammed a fallen branch through to secure it.

"The worms are eating him," panted Elenna.

The wriggling creatures crawled over the trapped Beast. Tom saw one of them burrow inside Hecton's chest, leaving a tiny oozing tunnel. Another disappeared into his thigh.

But Hecton's eyes flashed and he squirmed beneath the net. "None can defeat me," he snarled. "Prepare to die."

With a hiss, he punched forwards with his trident, slicing a gash through the net. It collapsed around him and he leaped free, the rotting cloak spread out behind him. Elenna aimed an arrow at the Beast but his movements were too quick, and it fell uselessly to the ground.

Tom grabbed his shield and braced himself against the charging Beast. Hecton thrust his trident towards Tom's chest, but Tom deflected the blow with a swipe of his sword. The ringing clash of metal echoed through the trees. Hecton grabbed the edge of his cape, making the creatures stitched into it give a high-pitched moan. The sound sent a chill down Tom's spine.

"You will become one of them," Hecton yelled. He swung the cape at Tom, trying to envelop him in its gruesome folds. Pus flicked from the creatures' bodies, raining on Tom in thick yellow blobs. The slick surface of the cape skimmed over him and Tom gave a cry of revulsion. He held his breath against the stench and dropped to the ground, rolling free. Hecton swung the cape at him again, but a zipping arrow from Elenna thudded into his shoulder. The Beast howled with rage and Tom leapt aside.

I've got to trap Hecton inside that cape, Tom realised, shaking the slime from his hands.

As Hecton lifted his cape and swooped at him, Tom stepped to the left. Hecton followed, but Tom sprang to the right instead. The cape swirled through empty air then wrapped around the Beast. He tried to struggle out, but the sticky insides of the cape seemed to suck up to his skin, the rotting bodies of all those caught animals smothering him.

"No..." Hecton howled. The creatures' cries rose to a shrill scream of revenge, as if they were delighting in their victory over their master. The worms pushed into him until none of his green body remained. Hecton's eyes fixed on Tom then closed. The pile of worms collapsed, then with a final hiss of green mist, melted away into the ground.

Tom exhaled a long breath. He sank to the ground, exhausted. Elenna flopped down next to him. "We did it," Tom panted.

"I can't remember a more revolting Beast," said Elenna with a shudder.

She blinked suddenly. A raindrop slid down her face, leaving a clean trail through the sheen of ash. They

grinned at each other and looked up at the sky.

Fat raindrops splattered through the Vanished Woodland, washing the grey ash from the trees and leaving vibrant shades of green in its place.

Tom got up. "Sanpao's evil is leaving."

The rotting cape and trident lay on the patch of ground where Hecton had disappeared. Tom picked up the trident. It was too large to slide into his belt, so he slung it over his shoulder. "Hecton's token," he said. "We'll find out what powers it has soon enough."

A flash of movement caught Tom's eye. The cape was twitching. They stared, amazed, as a rabbit wriggled its way out. It sat still for a moment, its nose snuffling, then bounded into the undergrowth. Then the snout of a fox poked through the folds. It trotted away, swishing its brush. The creatures were coming back to life!

Elenna's eyes shone with wonder. "Hecton's evil is being reversed," she breathed.

The cape fizzed with sparks of red and purple light. Tom and Elenna ducked behind a bush so as not to startle the emerging creatures. Birds fluttered out, singing as they soared away. Mice scurried free and grass snakes slithered through the bushes, their tongues flickering. There was a low bellow and a magnificent bull thrust its way out. His muscular flanks shone and he tossed his head, his horns gleaming as he charged into the Woodland.

"His skull formed the hood of the cape," Tom remembered.

Elenna clutched his arm and pointed through the leaves at the final creature to emerge. But it wasn't a creature – it was a boy.

He was dressed in a tunic made of bark, his long hair tied back with a length of creeper. He rubbed his eyes and seized hold of a vine, hoisting himself up and swinging away through the branches.

"He must be a Tree Dweller," gasped Tom. "One of the people who

lives in those huts!"

The two friends made their way through the Vanished Woodland, back to where Storm and Blizzard would be waiting for them. Tom glanced over his shoulder for a final look at the Tree of Being. It was already sinking into the ground, its branches curled around its thick trunk as it drilled into the earth. Tom knew that it would soon emerge in a new location. The pirates would be waiting to capture it, but so would Tom. And the tree was getting stronger all the time – soon a portal would appear into the world where Freya and Silver were held prisoner, and Tom would have them back. But in the meantime...

Are you ready for our next battle, Sanpao? he thought. *I know I am.*

TOM'S QUEST CONTINUES IN

THE
PIRATE KING
COLLECTION
PART 2

Join the Quest,
Join the Tribe

www.beastquest.co.uk

Have you checked out the Beast Quest website?
It's the place to go for games, downloads, activities,
sneak previews and lots of fun!

You can read all about your favourite Beasts,
download free screensavers and desktop wallpapers
for your computer, and even challenge your friends
to a Beast Tournament.

Sign up to the newsletter at www.beastquest.co.uk
to receive exclusive extra content and the
opportunity to enter special members-only
competitions. We'll send you up-to-date info on all
the Beast Quest books, including the next exciting
series which features six brand-new Beasts!

Get 30% off all Beast Quest Books at www.beastquest.co.uk
Enter the code BEAST at the checkout.

All books priced at £4.99.
Special bumper editions priced at £5.99.

Orchard Books are available from all good bookshops, or can
be ordered from our website: www.orchardbooks.co.uk,
or telephone 01235 827702, or fax 01235 8227703.